By the same author

Adult Titles

The Pushbutton Butterfly
The Kissing Gourami
Dead As They Come
The Princess Stakes Murder

Juvenile Titles

The Blue Man
Big Max
Sinbad and Me
The Boy Who Could Make Himself Disappear
Mystery of the Witch Who Wouldn't
Hey Dummy
Chloris and the Creeps

The Giant Kill

The Giant Kill

Kin Platt

Random House: New York

Library of Congress Cataloging in Publication Data

Platt, Kin.
  The giant kill.

  I. Title.
PZ4.P7196Gi [PS3566.L29]   813'.5'4   73-16396
ISBN 0-394-48707-9

Manufactured in the United States of America
by the Colonial Press Inc., Clinton, Mass.
9 8 7 6 5 4 3 2
First Edition

To Malachi Lee, twentieth-century *ninja*

The Giant Kill

One

My arms were loaded with groceries Sunday evening when I got back to my apartment. The two men inside wore comic masks, one a gorilla, the other a rube. The gorilla showed me the gun in his hand, and I knew right away it was too early for Halloween. The third man was behind the door. I never got the chance to see what he was wearing, but he was carrying something heavy. My head got in the way of its downward arc.

The room was going up and down when I opened my eyes. Then it shifted to a side-to-side shimmy and I noticed something else that was odd about it. There were pictures on the wall. Paintings. It wasn't my room. Seagulls screeched over my head and there was the smell of the sea. I blinked and saw a few people. They were going up and down, too, along with the room, and I wondered what I was doing on a boat.

I was sitting braced on a chair, my arms behind me, wrists lashed tightly together. The gorilla man was blocking out my left side. The rube was on the right. A strong light flashed out of the darkness, hung on my sweating face, and I heard a man talking. "Gonzaga," he said. "I want Gonzaga."

The only Gonzaga I know is three inches or so over seven feet, comes in at close to three hundred pounds, and has been chronicled in the NBA record books as perhaps the greatest scoring machine basketball has ever known. Although he has been a part-time friend of mine for a lot of years, Gonzaga is his own man, and always has been. I couldn't give him to this man in the shadows even if I wanted to.

3

I tried explaining this in my usual witty fashion. The talking man stopped and the gorilla man belted me backhand across the chops. The rube held his position but the floor creaked under his feet and I knew he was lining himself up for the next cheap shot. I spit my blood across his shoes and he moved back a step.

"Hit me now so I can remember you," I told him. "If you want Gonzaga, I know you're not going to kill me. Maybe next time my hands won't be tied."

He let the air out of his lungs slowly and I waited for the jolt. The light went out suddenly and I heard the man's voice from across the shadowy room. "No, Lloyd." The rube sucked in air again. It took a little while to get to the top of his chest.

The man was speaking again. His voice was low and throaty. He had to have a short thick neck or he smoked and boozed a lot. The words came out blurry and singsong in an Eastern cadence. He needed diction lessons, but I had bigger problems.

"Listen to it all, Roper. I want Gonzaga not to play in the play-off series. You got that? It will be up to you to talk him out of it. If he plays, he's dead. If he plays, you're dead too."

"You're out of your head," I told him. "Why would Gonzaga listen to me? He's been in the game a long time. He's been approached by plenty of tinhorn gamblers before—"

It was as far as I got. They must have had their own signals. I sensed the quick movement behind me too late. I'd forgotten the third man again. His hand jerked my head back and something that could have been a heavy fist or a sixteen-pound-weight hit me behind the ear.

I didn't get his name. All I got was a headache. When I woke up I was back in my own room. It was going up and down and spinning just like the other one. But it was home and I felt a little better about it. My hands weren't tied together any more and I crawled toward the bag of groceries on the floor. I remembered bringing home some booze on my shopping trip, and how careful I was not to drop any bottles when the hoods with their funny faces braced me.

Two

Along with his other NBA records, Gonzaga was credited with the most assists by a center. His team play suffered over the telephone.

"Sorry I can't help you, Roper."

"Maybe you weren't listening. The man said if you played, you were dead."

"I've heard it before. You realize if we take the Knicks, that championship will be worth about twenty grand a man when we cut it up? That can buy a lot of bourbon."

"You'll be stiff a lot quicker the man's way."

"Thanks for the call," he said, chuckling. "You want a seat for the opening game tomorrow night?"

"If you're playing, yes."

"In your name at the box office. I figure we ought to take them in five games. What do you think?"

"Isn't that what you said last year?"

He laughed. "Last year nobody held a gun on my head. Maybe I'll shoot better."

I didn't get waspish about it. There was an outside chance the mystery man on the boat was bluffing. Knocking off a superstar like Jo-Jo Gonzaga wouldn't be that easy. Although he was a very private man, there was always the coterie surrounding him. There aren't too many seven-footers around with a two-million-dollar bachelor lean-to in the Santa Monica hills of Brentwood. Along with his legitimate admirers, there was always a swarm of leggy twiggies after him, a formidable ring not easily muscled away.

Apart from the lingering headache, all I had going for me on the line was a shadowy figure with a fortune-cookie background who used boats for his business meetings. Two hoods who liked to wear party masks. A third who was up there with the best in skull-bashing from behind. A hood named Lloyd.

I used up one of the twenty-four hours I had, laying it all out for my friend at Homicide, Detective-Lieutenant Camino. Camino isn't a Johnny-come-lately pig. He's been at it for nearly enough time to shove it all for a pension.

His hands weren't any bigger than a pair of coconuts, but he rubbed them together without drawing sparks. "Christ, it's cold this morning. Man on a boat, you say, with a funny way of talking. You didn't get any kind of look at him?"

I shook the old head. Nothing rattled or fell off. "I saw a man wearing a gorilla mask. About six-two, around two hundred. A shade less for Lloyd the rube. I wish I knew what the odd man behind looked like." I touched the back of my head. It still hurt. "He must be a big guy. Hits pretty hard."

Camino nodded unsympathetically. "Could be your skull is a lot softer than it used to be. You've been catching a lot lately. What happened to all that karate?"

"Some hoods don't play fair. They don't give me a chance to use it."

Camino broke open a pack of chewing gum. He smokes in between the sticks he chews to break one habit or the other. "It's at least fifteen minutes from your apartment in Santa Monica to the nearest marina docking area. I don't like your being knocked out for that long."

"I don't like it either," I said. The long kayo had puzzled me too.

"Then you get another rap from behind on the boat and you don't wake up until you're back in your apartment. You don't wake up in the car either trip."

"I told you," I whined. "That guy hit hard."

"Maybe you ought to have your head examined," Camino said.

6

"It's my job," I said. "Nobody forced me to become a private dick."

Camino smiled thinly. "That's not what I meant. Take your coat off."

"You want to fight me? Here in the squad room?"

He shook his head. "I don't fight any more. I don't have the energy. Take off your coat."

I shrugged and took off my coat.

Camino took the coat and dumped it in a chair. His chin jutted an extra inch. "Now the shirt."

I stared. "You're supposed to be a happily married man. When did you become mad about my body?"

Camino extended his hand. "The shirt."

I got up and gave him the shirt off my back. I looked down at my exposed torso, wondering if I had put on some flab Camino had somehow detected. I half turned, flexing both arms. "Just tell me the pose you want. I can send you pictures."

Camino snorted and got off his keester and walked around the desk. His eyes intently scanned my skin.

I made my eyes open wider. "Don't touch me or I'll call a cop," I said in a girlish treble.

Camino's finger jabbed my right arm. "This red spot. How long have you had it?"

I lifted my arm and tried to see the little red spot. "I didn't know I had a little red spot."

"You got one now."

"Measles?"

Camino smiled mirthlessly. "You didn't feel anything after you were slugged?"

"What's to feel?" I said. "You get slugged, the lights go out and you fall down."

Camino nodded. "Smart. That's why you never felt the needle."

My eyes widened on their own. "Needle?"

Camino turned back to his desk, bent over his phone and spun the dial. "Doc, Camino here. Can you come in?"

He dropped the phone back on its cradle, leaned against his desk and folded his arms. I was still trying to twist my arm and head past their limits when the door opened and Doc Shipman walked in.

"You remember Roper," Camino said.

"I've heard the name," Shipman said. He looked me over. "Is that his body?"

Camino took the wad of gum out of his mouth and inserted a cigarette. "Look at that red spot behind his right arm, Doc."

I lifted the arm and Shipman took a closer look. "It looks red," he said cautiously.

"We'd like a medical opinion," Camino said.

Doc Shipman cleared his throat. "For a red spot, he's supposed to consult his own physician. I work for the department."

"That's what I thought," Camino said. "Do some work for the department and tell us about that red spot Roper has."

Shipman took another look and stepped back. "So he's on the needle. I told Roper long ago booze wasn't good for him."

I looked at Shipman. Doc wasn't kidding. I looked at Camino. "What the hell is going on here?"

Camino ignored my question and laid it all out for the police medic. "Roper was slugged twice and went out cold for at least fifteen minutes each time. He claims he never felt any needle."

Doc nodded. "That's not surprising. He was unconscious each time when they slipped it into him."

"Slipped what into me?" I said, trying to keep up with the learned discussion.

"Did you smell anything when you woke up the first time?" Doc asked.

"Sea smells. I was on a boat."

"How about the second time—when you woke up in your own apartment?"

I tried to remember. "I think I still had it. Maybe I was on the boat longer than I thought."

Doc Shipman opened his black leather bag. He fumbled around inside and came up with a narrow colorless vial of liquid. He unscrewed the top and held it close to my nose. "Tell me what you smell?"

My nose wrinkled. "I smell a dastardly plot," I said and started getting dressed again. "What is that stuff?"

"One of the newer barbiturates I can't pronounce. But it does the job fast without side effects."

I slipped my coat on. "They were being careful. They wanted to be very sure I couldn't identify the area where their boat was tied up."

Doc Shipman grunted. His experienced fingers were deftly probing the back of my head. I winced only twice.

"With that quick-acting drug, they didn't have to slug you at all. Curious," he said.

"Very," I admitted. "Perhaps they've been seeing too many gangster movies."

Camino tossed his butt unerringly into the can in the corner. "That reminds me. If you ever catch up to that fellow Lloyd, don't kill him. I want a chance to talk to him."

I rubbed my upper arm. Now that I knew I'd been jabbed with a needle, it was beginning to hurt some. "I'll try not to. Gonzaga's going to play. What are you going to do about him?"

"We'll put a couple of men on him and see that he doesn't get hurt."

"Thanks," I said and started out.

"You're forgetting something," Camino said, and I stopped. "I thought the man told you if Gonzaga plays, you get killed too."

I snapped my fingers. "I forgot."

Three

I spun my wheels to the west-side marina. There were a lot of boats in the water. I eliminated all the little ones and tried to concentrate on the bigger jobs. There were too many of them; it was an affluent society. People were buying boats the way they used to buy hammocks. They were lapping them up for fifty to a hundred gees. Some used them instead of houses or apartments. The man I was looking for made it work as an office.

I tried to relax, home in on it the way the bats and birds do. It brought me to a dead end on Fiji Way. Dogs and cats had that special sense too. They could be blindfolded and make their way back over a thousand miles. I knew I wasn't a dog or cat, but I tried, anyway. It brought me to a liquor store in the middle of the marina. I had the wrong kind of radar working.

There were new restaurants and bars thrown up every few hundred yards. My abductors could have been drinking men; I tried the bars and looked around. I saw a lot of cute-looking dolls in long black stockings pushing their luck with trays.

I stopped one showing all the available assets. Her big green eyes widened and fastened greedily on the bill I waved. She came to a complete curving stop.

"Fellow named Lloyd. Come in here much?"

Her long hair flounced as her head wagged negative. "What does he look like?"

"About my size."

She took her time looking it over. "What does he do?"

"He hits people."

She backed up a step. Her low-cut blouse wasn't trying too hard to contain its secrets. "I don't know anybody like that, mister."

I dropped the bill on her tray. "Sometimes he travels with a friend."

She smiled, her eyes on the bill. "Thank you, sir. What does his friend look like?"

"Last time it was a gorilla."

The bar girls are used to all the Los Angeles nuts, but this one had a De Mille background. Her red lips opened but she didn't kiss me or scream for the paddy wagon. "No gorillas come in here, sir."

"Sometimes Lloyd and the gorilla team up with a third man."

"What's he like?" she asked patiently.

I sighed and fished another bill out for her interest. "I don't know yet."

"Anything else, mister?"

"One other man. Talks funny. Slurs his letters."

She sniffed. "I thought all men talked that way in bars after a few drinks."

"This one might be Hawaiian. Maybe Chinese."

"What's your friend's name?"

I let go of the bill. "I wish I knew."

She picked up the money. "I like the way you ask questions, mister. Drop in again sometime." She started away and stopped. "I could ask around. But you don't know enough names."

"I don't even know yours."

"Bunny. What's yours?"

I told her. "Give me a buzz any time you think those boys are in here."

"If it's the gorilla, he'll have to wear a tie."

I drifted to the other marina bars. No gorillas, rubes or singsong Orientals. The play-off opener at the Forum in Inglewood was due to start in a few hours. I was out of time.

Gonzaga's butler, Little Freddy, answered the phone. The big man had already left for the sports palace. I asked how Gonzaga felt.

"Cheery, man. Way up. We're gonna whomp those Knickers."

I patted the worry lines off my face, tied on my gun, and drove down to see the basketball game. There wasn't any way to guess which of us would be killed first.

The big mile-square parking lot was nearly filled when I gave the attendant my buck and parked the heap. The Lakers were saddled with a lot of disillusioned fans who had seen the home team blow it all every chance they had before. They were arriving early this night of the opener in order not to lose the opportunity of razzing that their seats provided, avid to show their scorn and root for the opposition instead. Angelenos were funny in many ways. Taunting their own representatives in the big intercity finale was merely another way.

I didn't see Camino around or any of his men. There was the usual sprinkling of cops, as at every sporting event, and the Forum had its own security detail. Normally, that would have been good enough for me, but this night I wanted tighter control, a little special extra-added effort.

A lanky red-headed man wearing the rumpled blue of the sports arena's security detail braced me with a thin ramrod arm. "Looking for somebody?"

I knew him as Tom Power, a former sharpshooting guard for the Lakers. Bad knees had forced him out of the line-up. He had bounced around the league, the knees didn't get better, and suddenly his playing days were over. He couldn't hack it coaching. He tried selling insurance, but that wasn't any go either, and he hit the skids.

It had been Power's bad luck along with a lot of others to have been good before the new breed of smart sports agents came in. They haggled better deals with management and started the glamorous trend of superstars and their stratospheric salaries. The flashy shooters like Chamberlain, Jabbar and Gonzaga became instant millionaires.

Power listened to what I had to tell him and looked down at me impassively from his six-four shelf of bushy red eyebrows. "Okay, Roper. I'll see to it nobody gets close to Gonzaga tonight. What gives?"

"A man doesn't want him to play."

He whistled a short note and straightened up. "Like that, huh?"

"We've got some fuzz planted in the crowd. Considering what Gonzaga's done for you, I figured you might do a better job."

Along with some of the things Gonzaga had done, was getting Power his job on the Forum security detail. When he learned the former Laker was on lean pickings, he got on the horn and persuaded the front office it needed another man watching over their palace grounds. While the job didn't pay enough to turn the taciturn redhead into a freewheeling big spender, it kept his family off welfare, paid his bills, and allowed him to stay pretty close to the game he loved. It also took him off the bar stools and boozing himself up to that big court in the sky where all the rim shots go in.

"I don't know if the hit is set for tonight or the next one," I said. I had learned my lesson with the bar bunny and didn't go into describing the faceless would-be killers. "Just keep your eyes open and watch the crowd, Tom."

Power patted the .38 on his hip. "Don't worry, Roper. I'll look after Jo-Jo all the way. I owe him plenty. Not only for the job here, but a lot you don't know about."

"Luck."

He waved nonchalantly, and I watched him walk away, carefully nursing the stride on his gimpy legs. Once he stopped, looking intently as a big black Continental swung into its parking space. A lovely broad stepped out, hiking down her short skirt an inch. She stared Power down, and he backed off, turned and sauntered toward the main entrance. I cursed him silently, hoping he would get his mind off the broads this night and stay on the track where I'd placed him.

I picked up my ticket at the box office. It was a good seat favoring the action, but I was afraid I'd get locked in watching the game and kept moving around. I didn't see any people wearing party masks, and the only funny faces they wore happened to be their own. The din was terrific and I couldn't single out any Oriental cheering for the opposition.

It was a tight game, but Gonzaga finally broke it open for the Lakers late in the third quarter. The Knicks held a 75–71 advantage with 2:29 left when Gonzaga put away three straight free throws and a lay-up, then converted a three-point play that put the Lakers in front to stay at 83–76. He scored thirty points and grabbed twenty-four rebounds, whirled in his hooks from twelve- to fifteen-foot range and he wasn't partial to any spot on the floor. He made eight of his first ten shots and had fifteen points at halftime. For a man expecting a bullet in his back, it wasn't a bad night's work.

There was the usual cordon of cops around the Lakers when they left, to protect them from their loyal fans, and although well covered from all sides, Gonzaga towered so over everybody, it would have taken a palsied marksman to miss that much of him. I reminded myself that tonight was supposed to be share-and-share-alike, and got in my car with my heater on my lap. Nobody tailed me or cut me off suddenly and I didn't have to play any games on the way home.

The phone rang at intervals throughout the night, and when I finally picked it up I had the tape hook-up ready.

"Hello. You Roper?"

The l's and r's made it on their own. I wondered why I had tagged him as an Oriental. I watched the little tapes spin silently and told him yes, I was Roper. "How did you like the game?" I asked.

"Smart guy. We let this one go. We see how smart you feel tomorrow."

"How about Gonzaga? Is he going to feel smart too?"

My friend with the strange cadence chuckled softly. "Gonzaga bigger fool than you. He not gonna feel anything, because he gonna be pretty quick dead."

There was a click and the phone went dead in my hand. I spun back the tape and listened to it again. I didn't have a record of our first conversation, but something had changed. He was laying on the patois this time, mangling the language like a refugee from a rickshaw. I wondered about it and fell asleep.

14

Four

It wasn't any wilder than a trip to another planet. The architect had parlayed a simple circle into a towering ring-shaped surrealistic dream he got out of Babel. For a cool two million, it guaranteed the owner wouldn't bump his head any place. The fifteen-foot sculptured bronze door was as lovingly designed as the Gate of Ishtar. It could hold three hundred people without them rubbing elbows. The chimney was a fifty-foot white-stone tower, the master bathroom was lined with gold tile, the bathtub a huge sunken mosaic pool. The guest room was wall-to-wall crimson plush lined with custom-built sofas covered in llama skin surrounding a huge circular bed. It had psychedelic lighting, gold-edged mirrors, and you had to remove your shoes to enter it.

Gonzaga's bedroom occupied the upper floor. It had sides of angled mirrors, more psychedelic lighting, the circular bed could have contained a harem, and the man in it, while doing without one for the moment, appeared to be considering the prospect.

"It's cozy," I said. "I hope you can keep playing so you can afford to pay the taxes."

Gonzaga laughed. "It's worth every nickel. Watch!" His hand flicked a button on an electronic panel. The tiled ceiling over the huge bed rolled back silently, revealing the sky. "The air is great up here. Take a whiff."

"Around my neighborhood, it's free."

Gonzaga wrinkled his nose disdainfully. "Don't be plebian, man. How about a drink?"

He touched another button on the control panel. A portable bar against the far wall started to move. "Hurry it up there!" Gonzaga roared, hitting another button. The bar didn't argue and zipped up to us, clinking gently. It was a dipso's dream, loaded with bottles of every drink known to man.

Gonzaga watched me pour some of his good stuff. "What's under your arm—a present?"

"You might call it that. If you don't play tonight."

Gonzaga slid his bare feet into a set of white mink slippers. They couldn't have set him back more than a month's pay. He lifted his huge powerful arms, yawning as he stretched. "Isn't it too early to be serious, man?"

"Not if you like presents. This sounds like a good one."

"Sounds like?" He pulled the tape out of the box. "I hope it's none of that happy-birthday jazz."

I let more of his smooth Scotch roll down. "Press one of your magic buttons and play it. Maybe with luck you might live to see your next birthday."

He frowned and his swarthy face was menacing and ugly. "Shit, man, you're not kidding, are you?"

"Play it, Sam," I said. "It's our song."

He flipped open a cabinet and played the tape. He listened quietly, shut it off and spun it back. He lifted it off and held it in thick fingers, moody-eyed and angry. "I didn't know you were in it with me. Sorry."

I shrugged. "Point one—do you know the voice?"

Gonzaga shook his head. "A Chinese hood. Threatening me?" His voice thundered incredulity. His fingers tightened on the spool.

I held out my hand. "Don't rip it. Maybe I can trace the voice. Camino may know somebody."

Gonzaga sniffed. "Yeah, man. That'll do us both good. Well, I heard it all before and now I'm hearing it one more time. We gotta win. I'm goin' all out tonight. You know that. We're gonna sink those Knicks, and we won't need all seven games to do it. You hear me?"

The sound of baying outside brought me to the window. Gonzaga's finger tapped the pane. "I got these two Great Danes.

16

Anybody comes here looking for me gonna get a nice reception."

"Swell," I said. "There were four of them, by the way. The man on the tape. The three hoods who tapped me out and brought me out to see him on his boat."

Gonzaga snickered. "Boat? This cat's got a boat? He does his business on a boat?" His big brown eyes rolled to the corners of his big spread. "What kind of boat?"

"Maybe it was a yacht," I said. "I wasn't awake long enough to notice the details."

"Tough," Gonzaga said. He was silent a moment, then pointed down again toward the dogs. "You can stay here if you want." He waved his arms expansively. "Plenty of room. Plenty of booze. Plenty of broads."

"It doesn't have to be here, Jo-Jo. It doesn't have to be at the Forum either. If they're on the level, it can be any place."

Gonzaga grinned, showing a lot of ivory. "Well, screw 'em. That's what I say."

"That's what I say, too." I set my glass down. "Make some of those free throws tonight. You might need them."

"Shit, man. I'm gonna make 'em all."

He reached out and pressed a magic button. The overhead tile slid over and blotted out the sky.

Little Freddy let me out the big front door. "You watch us tonight," he crowed. "We gonna really blitz them Knicks. Ain't that what the big fellow said?"

"That's about what he said," I said.

Gonzaga's Big Danes looked curiously at me from their pen as I walked out. It was good to know they figured I was a friend.

Camino had a real-life murder on his hands and couldn't give me much time with the tape. "Leave it," he barked, "and I'll get a few people to listen to it. I got no time to play guessing games now. When they knock you off, I'll give you the same preference."

"When they knock me off, I won't need any favors."

"Say, that's right. Then watch yourself and do me a favor

and get the hell out of here. Make it tomorrow, if you're still living."

"I'll try to remember that."

I cruised around and discovered nothing. I couldn't find the boat in the marina and the harbor master wasn't in his office. Nobody knew of any Oriental boat owners.

I burned a lot more rubber around the marina and my throat on an assortment of bad bar booze. It was getting late when I figured the hell with it and headed down the pike for the Forum in Inglewood.

I looked around for Tom Power and couldn't find him. I ordered a good dinner in the house restaurant but my mind wasn't on it. The drinks were better here and I lingered over the last of them and then made myself get up and walk around.

Power tapped me from behind. He paled and backed up frightened when he realized what he'd done. My gun was up and an inch away from his belly.

"Sorry," I said. "Maybe you better find another way to say hello."

His pale face flushed as he followed my eyes down to the gun at his hip. He knew suddenly the feelings of a rotten security guard. "Christ!" He licked his lips. "I—I didn't mean anything."

"All right. Same instructions as last night. Keep your eyes open."

A whining note came into his voice. "For what? What the hell am I looking for? How the hell do you know who's planning to kill somebody?" He patted perspiration from his face with a soggy rumpled handkerchief. "This is your racket, you know. I'm a basketball player. Don't let the uniform fool you."

I smiled. "It won't. They may come in one car. Four men."

The Adam's apple bobbed and seemed stuck in his throat. "F-four?"

"Three big guys."

"Oh, yeah? What's the other one like?"

"I don't know. But he's got a kind of singsong voice. Maybe Chinese."

"That's all you got on them?"

"That's it. You don't have to take them on yourself. If you spot them, let me know. Or tell it to some of the fuzz. They're in on the picture."

Power put his thumb on his middle finger and showed me the circle. "A-okay. Gotcha, pal."

I watched his long lanky form drift away until he was lost in the crowd of incoming fans. I checked my rose-colored seat before taking it. There weren't any bombs underneath. The organist began working on the anthem and the crowd got to its feet. There were seventeen thousand fans here for the second game of the play-off. Power was right. You couldn't guess the killer just looking at them.

Gonzaga took the jeers he was accustomed to along with scattered applause at the intros. He stood up straight, with his fists jammed on his hips, smiling. His eyes had a devilish glint. A light sweat glistened on his swarthy giant frame. He stood reflecting awesome power bigger and stronger than all the other big men around him.

He didn't waste any time when the game started, hustling down the court, blocking out the shots and grabbing all the rebounds off the boards. He handed off and when nobody was available turned and floated in his own little finger rolls and hook shots. On defense, his physical presence jarred and deflected the Knick attack. His steamshovel hands blocked everything in sight. Again he was in double figures at the half.

The Knicks challenged again in the third quarter, Lucas looping in high twenty-five-foot shots over Gonzaga's head. But the Lakers spurted behind Gonzaga, moving quickly and finding the open man. They held off the rallying Knicks in the final period and won it 111–107. Gonzaga picked up thirty-two points and thirty-one rebounds. He ran seven straight from the foul line. It was obviously his inspiring defensive play that blunted and finally broke the Knick attack, cementing the Laker win. The moody big man was showing his contempt for the mystery man's threat.

I waited at the head of the tunnel, checking out the crowd of waiting fans. Nobody was fingering a holster. Gonzaga came out after showering, surrounded again by a tightly drawn cordon of blue-shirted fuzz. His face gleamed as he grunted curt responses to the win-happy fans. He wasn't about to forgive them for their jeers on other nights. He saw me, grinned and waved his hamlike fist. "Did we show those mothers?" he yelled.

I found my heap, and nothing blew up when I turned the starter over. The teams would now play the next two games at the Garden in New York. I wasn't that dedicated a fan, but I was in this one up to my ears and knew I had to tag along.

Camino woke me at four in the morning.

"Gonzaga's dead. Shot four times. You okay?"

Five

It had been a small catered party. Every corner had its own bar. Mounds of food cascaded from tables in the dining rooms. They were rich with hot and cold hors d'oeuvre. Seafood delicacies were piled in lopped-off pyramids. Shrimp and crab claws rumaki, Hawaiian chicken, egg rolls and beef were set alongside dishes of pepper steak and fried rice.

I found Camino upstairs.

"It could have come from anywhere out there." He spat over the terrace ledge angrily. "It was a high-powered rifle. With one of those, they could have knocked Gonzaga off from the Freeway."

The crescent-shaped terrace on the second floor overlooked the landscape of the Santa Monica mountains. Brentwood had been Gonzaga's front yard, as the San Fernando Valley was the back. The two-million dollar five-acre showplace had its own built-in weakness. The architect had been preoccupied with his three-ringed motif. He hadn't given a thought to assassins in the night shooting from below.

"I suppose he was out here taking another look at his spread," I told Camino. "That, or flexing his chest."

Camino stared. "What?"

"The air is pretty good up here. You know, he has that ceiling mirror over his bed electronically controlled. He can roll it back to take a deep breath of fresh air when he needs it."

"He *had*," Camino said viciously. "Why the hell didn't he

stay in bed and play with his gadgets last night? Why give the shooter out there an easy target?"

Camino was snarling because he had been fond of Gonzaga. I let him steam, getting it out of his system.

"He had a party going," I said. "Lots of people downstairs. Maybe it was too early for him to be in bed."

Camino's lip curled. "With all that talent waiting downstairs? What the hell difference would it make what time it was?"

I shrugged. "Anything on the tape I left you?" Time ran out for Gonzaga so far as he was concerned.

"Nobody could come up with a thing." Camino put his hand in his pocket and came out with the tape. "I'm sending you over to see a broad."

It wasn't like the man to break his own continuity. I nodded, waiting. He pulled out his notebook, scribbled over a page, ripped it off and gave it to me.

His scrawl wasn't any harder to decipher than a doctor's prescription. "Sandy Shaw?"

"She's some kind of hot-shot science whiz kid out at UCLA. She and this professor she teams up with have something going with a new process identifying voice patterns. Maybe she can break your mystery caller down for you."

"Voice patterns? You mean voice prints?"

"Whatever the hell they call it," Camino said, sounding hard and hostile. "Get your ass over there. Maybe you two with your big brains can work it out together."

"Maybe." I pocketed the slip of paper and looked around the giant-sized room, my brows knitting.

"What's bugging you?" asked Camino.

I looked up at the twenty-foot-high ceiling, then back to the Judas terrace. "It's all too neat and tidy. Gonzaga weighed at least two-seven-oh during the playing season. A big powerful man. The way it looks here, he got hit four times and just laid down and died."

Camino nodded. "What's your point?"

"Seems like perfect timing. Someone knew his habits. That he liked to step out on his little terrace and look around."

Camino shrugged. "Okay, so they were waiting for him to step outside. Anything else?"

"Apart from it looking too neat and tidy, I don't know."

Camino snorted, lit a butt and tossed the match over the edge of the terrace. "The bullets were .404 Magnum. They'd stop a rhino or elephant dead in its tracks. Gonzaga was only a man."

"Mauser sporting rifle?"

"Had to be a big game gun. We haven't found it yet. I've got some men out there beating the bush."

The Mauser is ideally suited for bagging large and dangerous game. The rear sight is graduated up to a thousand yards. Mounted with a telescopic sight, it's a weapon guaranteed to do its work. The magazine holds five cartridges.

"You said four hits. Any sign of a miss?"

Camino shook his head. "How could anybody miss a man that size? What's eating you now?"

I looked out toward the misty hills. "He's still got a shot left. Maybe you ought to get off that terrace."

Camino rocked back on his heels, his face set in stubborn lines. "That'd be the day," he said coldly. "Why don't you get the hell out of here and talk to that voice-print hot shot and let me take a bullet if I feel like it?"

I left him standing there, staring bleakly out toward the distant mountain ridge, defying the big bullet.

Gonzaga's Great Danes weren't in their pen. As I got into my heap, I heard them baying in the distance. If the killer knew Gonzaga's life style and habits, he'd know about the big dogs too. There wasn't much of a chance he'd be hanging around waiting. I felt glad, in a way. There would be something left for me.

The UCLA campus at Westwood was colorful and alive with the kids. The girls looked sloppier than ever but they were still very attractive. A lot of new young breasts had been liberated by the no-bra movement and it was difficult to fault such beguiling freedom. The longhairs flaunted their own tresses with equal bravado, and unless you knew where to look, some of those guys could really fool you.

23

My random window-shopping cooled rapidly when I came to the science wing of one of the newer buildings that had mushroomed on the sprawling campus. The architecture was severely geometric. The long corridor was cool and deserted. A large rectangular black card said in white lettering: LA SALLE. Tacked under it was a beat-up reversed calling card. Handwritten on it was *Shaw*. I pulled out the tack and reversed the card and Earle's Mobil station in Westwood was telling me its address and phone number. I set it straight, knocked, turned the big brass knob and walked in.

The room was large, quiet and devoid of frills, including the girl sitting behind a paper-strewn desk. She wore amber-rimmed glasses and carried more than a decent handicap of freckles. Her hair was so ragged, it could have been cut by a knife and fork. Morning sunlight accented the gold sheen.

"Miss Shaw? Sandy Shaw?"

She smiled, revealing the kind of teeth they like to model in the TV toothpaste commercials. Trapped and beguiled by an odd atavistic response, I found comfort and trust in those strong and straight white teeth. She bobbed her head and chewed on her lower lip, and seemed about to identify herself when a man came out from behind a tall metal console.

"I'm Dr. La Salle." He sounded nasal and annoyed. "What is it?"

I checked the scrap of paper I had bearing Camino's scrawl. "Sorry, but my business is with Miss Shaw."

His heavy black eyebrows lowered, and the girl stood up hesitantly, flushing. Her freckles disappeared. She looked very young. Although she wore a stiff lab smock, it was apparent immediately that she had more interesting features than shining white teeth. "I'm Sandy Shaw," she said in a tinkly little-girl voice. "But this is Dr. La Salle's office. I only assist—"

La Salle waved his hand, and she stopped. "Who are you? What do you want?"

"My name is Roper. I'm an investigator. I understand Miss Shaw does voice prints—"

"What kind of investigator?" he asked.

"Private," I said, knowing the reaction.

He sniffed, making me a winner. "Oh. That."

"It has its moments," I said lightly. "Maybe not up there with brain surgery, but we don't lose as many clients."

La Salle sniffed again and looked disdainful. He had Omar Sharif eyes, a full head of carefully brushed hair, a pale moon face and thin bloodless lips. He was so good-looking, he could have been gay.

I turned to the blond freckle-faced kid, who wasn't quite as pretty but looked more fun. "Lieutenant Camino of Homicide told me you might be able to pinpoint a voice I have on tape. It's police business, too, in a way."

"Then why aren't the police here?" asked La Salle acidly.

"They're too busy right now," I said.

"So are we," La Salle snapped. "And if our local police feel they can intrude upon us whenever they feel like it, with whoever they care to refer to us to cover their incompetence—"

I looked him over without putting a dent in his pose. "It was supposed to be a courtesy call," I said. "Of course, if you'd rather deal with the police directly and discuss their incompetence—"

The shaggy-haired girl cleared her throat and broke in. "I'm sure Dr. La Salle wouldn't mind really, if he thought we could help you." She glanced at La Salle appealingly. "It might not take long," she added, "and I did tell Lieutenant Camino to call on us any time if he had a problem in our field."

La Salle thought about it. I could imagine him checking over the dinner tab, saying no, he didn't have the cheesecake, he only had coffee, Herbert had the cheesecake.

"What's it about—some obscene phone call?"

"Not exactly. A man was killed."

"Who?"

"A basketball player. Jo-Jo Gonzaga of the Laker team."

"Oh. That big stud."

I didn't want to hit him because there was an outside chance I might still need his help. I looked down at the spool of tape in my hand wishing Gonzaga would give me a sign from the great beyond.

25

The little blond shaggy-haired assistant cut in quickly. "How awful!" She turned to La Salle. "Would you mind, Doctor La Salle? Perhaps I can help. I've finished the other reports."

La Salle shrugged his meaty shoulders. He picked up some papers, slid them into a manila folder, and smiled thinly in my direction. "Remind Lieutenant Camino this is still my office and my project." He leaned close to the girl, pinning her arm to his, whispered into her ear, and pecked her lightly on the cheek. "I'll be in the lab," he told her and walked out.

She took it calmly, showing the merest trace of color. I had to assume doing voice-print work was as dull as any other job and you had to get your kicks some way in a science room. She rubbed her arm when the door snicked closed. "I'm sorry. Dr. La Salle can be very difficult, at times. But this is his project. I'm merely assisting here to get credit for my master's."

"You'll get it," I said. "Maybe Camino didn't understand the setup here."

"Well," she said shyly, "several weeks ago Dr. La Salle was out with a head cold. Lieutenant Camino called here about a problem and I was here and able to help him with it, I think."

"Identifying a voice on tape?"

"Yes. Some friend of his was being bothered—one of those nuisance callers, you know—the usual thing, and the telephone company suggested we had better facilities to deal with it. It's all Dr. La Salle's work, though, it's his field."

"You only help out?"

"Well, yes." Her restless hands brushed away wisps of hair, then tugged at her short frock, trying without success to mask her curves. She needed more buttons or a flatter framework. "He's been the pioneer in the field," she added. "The computer is largely his own breakthrough. He's very good at mechanical aspects. I'm, well"—she smiled shyly—"more intuitive."

She flattened her skirt to her hips with quick brushing motions of her hands. This was a very sexy girl assistant, and I could understand La Salle distrusting visiting males. "What's the line called?" I asked.

"Phonemics. The analysis of sounds."

"Fine," I said, handing her the tape. "Analyze this one."

She took the tape, turned to the large slick console and set it up on a turntable. I watched her adjust various dial settings. She had great legs, and I was grateful Camino had recommended her instead of La Salle. She rolled out some graph paper, adjusted an overhead movable arm holding a stylus, pressed control buttons and slipped in a slotted form card.

"We'll run it through for regional and generic patterns," she told me. "It's always fun for me if I can outguess the computer."

She let the tape spin, leaning back with folded arms, giving the soft filtered voice all her concentration. Her blue eyes widened and swung to mine at the threat. She let it all run through, then rewound and played it again. "Is that all you have?"

"Yes. The first time I heard him speak in person. He didn't use the fractured English that time. I made him out as Oriental —Hawaiian or Chinese. This time on the tape he seemed to be putting it on for me."

Her eyes were thoughtful. "They do that at times on a follow-up call, in case there is a listening device, trying to change their speech pattern. But they really can't, you know. Their generic origins can't be disguised."

"Maybe not," I said. "But Camino sent me here because his detective division experts couldn't come up with anything."

"Jeepers!" she said. "They really must be awfully busy, like you said. I can't believe it. This one is so obvious."

"Maybe they don't have your intuition."

She grinned, picked up a pad and wrote across a page. "Let's see if I can beat the La Salle computer." Before I could say I couldn't care less about her games, her outstretched hand hit the console control button. The sleek machine whirred, groaned, made a lot of funny noises, and coughed out a small white slotted card.

The shaggy-haired kid ignored it, letting it lie there on the out-slot, and closed her eyes. "Subject born in southern province of China," she said dreamily. "Perhaps Yunnan. Has spent many years in Laos, and more recently in the northeast corner of Burma."

I reached for the computer card. It read: *So. China. Laos. Burma. Thailand.*

"You can open your eyes," I said. "You know more about it than the machine."

Her eyes snapped open. "No kidding?" She grabbed for the card, read it and bobbed her head. "Well," she said apologetically, "it's only a machine, remember. It can only deal in generalities." She winked merrily. "That's why I'm so valuable around here."

"How come?" I asked. "What's your secret?"

"Intuition," she said. "Also, my father was a professor of Eastern languages in China, Burma and Thailand. I was raised there."

"Here's to intuition," I said.

"If you care to wait, I'm sure Dr. La Salle would be willing to give you his best educated guess on your tape."

"I'll take yours," I said. "You use a better toothpaste."

She giggled and reached for the tape. "I suppose you want this."

I waved it off. "Better leave it here for now. Lieutenant Camino may want to call La Salle to get his opinion. I've got all I need."

She bobbed her head in agreement. "By the way," she said, "now that you more or less have your mystery voice typed, what's your next move? I've always been interested in private-eye stuff."

I stared into her guileless eyes. "It's simple," I said. "When I find him, I kill him." Her eyes widened and her lips parted. She was very young, and I tried hard to find the words to set her straight. "It's not a fun game. I needed an expert reading the tape so I wouldn't be making any mistake. Camino liked Gonzaga, too, and that's why he sent me over. He wouldn't want me killing the wrong guy, either."

When I left, her mouth was still hanging open. My head was whirling busily on another track. The Golden Triangle.

The documents and logbooks at the Narcotics Bureau read like a Hollywood script. Operations Blackjack, Condor and Eagle. The French, Latin-American and Chinese connections. The new drug threat came from the northeast corner of Burma which borders China, Laos and Thailand. The whole area, including parts of Thailand and Laos, is a no-man's land called the Golden Triangle because of the estimated seven hundred tons of opium produced there annually. About eight hundred tons of opium slips in from Burma alone, most of it from territory which the local opium king rules like a feudal lord.

Even if blondes sometimes lie, I know computers don't.

Six

The offices of EPT are deceptively ordinary-looking. Housed in a nondescript building on Wilshire below the so-called Miracle Mile, listed in the lobby directory as E-Z Percussion Tools, it conveys the aura of a down-at-the-heels business headed ineluctably toward rack and ruin. The outer fringes of offices are run by gray-haired old ladies who could pass for refugees from Pasadena and the encroached smog belt. They file things and answer the phone softly and take breaks for tea. They work in nine-to-five shifts and gossip, and if they are aware of what goes on inside, they show no signs of it.

Behind the sham front is the heart of it. The computers and efficiency. Fast-talking, fast-thinking alert women, labs, intelligence people, and the man who dreamed it all up, the Director of Intelligence without peer, O. J. Burr.

O.J. stands six-four, is thin, wide-shouldered, diffident and knowledgeable. He worked his track during the war with Intelligence, later was summoned to Washington and given the whole route to cover as Deputy Director of Intelligence for that big outfit on E Street with its own formidable three-lettered jig.

Eventually he tired of the heavy-handed government operation and came West to start his own baby. EPT. It meant Emergency Procedure Terminus, the end of the line for trouble. It was O.J.'s private cloak-and-dagger line, with his own hand-picked men. EPT worked with big business, the police, and government agencies when they wanted behind-the-scenes work which wouldn't backfire in their faces. It wasn't always clean, honest work, but that's the name of the game. The bad guys were always out there showing their muscle, and we were paid to hit back. We had weapons and were allowed to use them, and if we got shot up first, we tried to live.

Smith was our man in charge of narcotics, a former U.S. agent, a slightly built man with an impressive mustache. He didn't leap off his chair when I mentioned the Golden Triangle, but he cracked his knuckles, twirled the hairpiece under his nose, set the ends at a military angle, and got off his butt at last to fetch his file.

In June and July, Thai and U.S. narcotics agents had crossed over the Burma border and seized 3,853 kilograms of raw opium, 212 of morphine base, 453 of prepared smoking opium and seven of No. 4 pure heroin. A kilogram is 2.2 pounds. In two days the agents seized opium and opiates which would make half a ton of heroin. Prices rise sharply the farther down the pipeline the stuff moves. If that amount of heroin were to get to the United States, it could be worth $250 million at street value.

An estimated 6.5 to 10 tons of heroin are consumed annually in the United States. Equated roughly, that's between 65 and 100 tons of crude opium, the base for refined heroin.

Total worldwide production of illicit opium comes to about 1,300 metric tons. Approximately 700 tons of this are produced in the Golden Triangle area of Southeast Asia. The Middle East and Central Asia chip in about 1,700 tons of raw opium supposedly produced for legitimate medical purposes. The remainder comes from Turkey, 50 tons; Pakistan, 100 tons; Afghanistan, 100 tons; India, 250 tons.

I handed the file back to Smith. "What's the latest figure on heroin addicts in this country?"

He knew it by heart. "Six hundred thous and going up."

"Who's the big man in the Golden Triangle operation?"

He smiled and showed me the seat near his desk. "Rest the bones. This one will take a while."

It didn't take more than a half-hour. When I left, I knew a lot more about the man in Asia. A mysterious Chinese operating in the mountains of northern Burma in the Golden Triangle area. Narcotics agents had him down as Lo Hsinghan. His sanctuary was in Tachilek, a small Burmese town just across the Thai border. He had dealers making the runs to Saigon, Bangkok and Hong Kong.

Lo had a private army of at least 1,000 men composed of Dacoits, hill tribesmen, Yunnanese, Haws, Shans and deserters from the 93rd Kuomintang Division thrown out of China when the Communists took over in 1949.

His troops had modern weapons. American-made M-16 rifles, grenade launchers and mortars sold originally to the Lao army, black-marketed into Thailand. His fighting force was so good, the Burmese army was afraid to tackle it.

Lo had a lucrative border trade smuggling everything from bolts of cloth to truck engines into Burma in the black market created by the Burmese nationalization program.

The intelligence reports my associate Smith had me read said Lo bought his opium from hill farmers, transported it to his own refineries by mule caravan and pack horse. His troops provided the armed escort to prevent hijacking from rivals.

In Tachilek, Lo had a refinery complex where he produced morphine, smoking heroin and No. 1 heroin.

I took it all to my mentor and boss, O. J. Burr.

"Was your friend Gonzaga a pusher or dealer?" he asked.

"No more than I."

"The voice-print expert identified your mystery caller as coming from the same locale as this man Lo?"

"Yes. Right on the nose. Yunnan Province. Burma. Laos."

"Surely you can't believe this man Lo has now transported himself here to fix basketball games?"

"No, sir. That dumb, hopefully, I am not."

O.J. frowned and looked severely down the long slope of his nose. "An aide, perhaps?"

"I'd like to think so."

"The men with your man were also Chinese?"

"I don't know. He called one Lloyd."

"Inconsequential."

I nodded agreement. The man was never wrong. "There appears to be no connection. Where would you suggest I begin?"

O.J. shook his head negligently and sadly. "That is no question for you to ask, Max. You already have begun."

"I have?"

The heavy eyebrows lowered, followed instantly by his eyelids. "The beginning is all that puzzles you. Pay it no mind. Obviously, it is out of sequence."

"Yes, sir," I said.

His eyes opened and fixed steadily upon mine. "You still have your street connections?"

"Yes, sir," I said.

"Pursue them," O.J. said.

"I'll do that," I said. "And I'll chase those villains through hell and high water."

O.J. nodded. "Mexico might be a better idea." His hands reached for a folder on his desk. "I'll expect you to have your resolution within a week." He opened the manila folder. It concerned another matter. This meeting was over.

"Yes, sir," I said. "Will do!"

Having a deadline is always an inspiring thought.

Seven

I put in a last-chance call to Little Freddy to find out if anybody had been leaning on Gonzaga before the play-off games. The man from Burma with the Chinese inflection might have started it all from a different angle.

"No way," the once-happy little man told me. "Ain't nobody tried. A big man like Jo-Jo, who you gonna find want to lean on him, anyway? He could pick up any two, three or more full-size men if he felt like it and tear them apart while they was off the ground." The phone went silent and I could picture him shaking his head. "Man, you ought to know that," he added sadly when he came on again.

"I'm talking about another kind of leaning, Freddy. Say some big operators blew into town and they figured Gonzaga had a lot of good connections. Maybe they thought he would introduce them into the circle. Help them push off some of their product."

Little Freddy's voice was shrill. "You talkin' *shit*, man? You talkin' drugs? Hell, Jo-Jo hated that bind. Ain't nobody would take a chance talkin' to him about that kind of action. Least-ways, nobody who knew big G."

"This man wouldn't be afraid, Freddy. He carried a lot of muscle around. Maybe he called up the house sometime. You'd remember his voice. Even if he called one time, it would be important."

"What's his name?"

"I don't know. He's from China. He speaks English okay but it's singsong. You know where he's from."

"No, sir. Of course, Mister Jo-Jo he had all kinds of friends talking any which-way language. But they was all his friends. You figure this China man was the one shot down my boss?"

"He's my bet so far, Freddy. I don't have anybody else. He was the man who told me Gonzaga wasn't to play against the Knicks in the opener. If he did, he was betting his life on it."

Strangely, Little Freddy laughed. "He told you that? Why, that man is crazy. Don't make no difference if he from China or not. Ain't nobody living who don't know there ain't no way to put the fear into Mister Jo-Jo. Everybody know that. He one man way up above it all." He cackled again. "Somebody told you that, you got yourself one helluva crazy man. Say, don't you remember what happened to those fellers asked Jo-Jo to dump a game for them some years back? He tore them apart, he broke them into little pieces, you remember that."

I remembered.

"You say this singsong man from China did it, huh? That what you telling me?"

"He's all I've got so far."

Little Freddy mouthed some choice obscenities. "Too bad Mister Jo-Jo didn't let them big doggies loose the night we having the party. They'd sure made chop suey outta that China man hangin' out there in the dark with his big gun."

I had to agree. "Maybe it will come to mind later," I told him. "Any visitor who might have been there recently. Any one who might have made him the kind of business offer to make him mad, Freddy. You call me, Freddy. It's important."

He hooted into my earpiece. "You got to be kidding. You know everybody likes Jo-Jo. Ain't nobody fool enough to want to make him mad."

I hung up, knowing in my own mind there was that exception. He wasn't afraid of me and Gonzaga put together. His was the initial advantage, operating out of the dark with his private muscle, off a seemingly untrackable backwater boat. The original threat had included me as well as Gonzaga. With the Mexican giant down now and out of the play, I wondered about his next move. The Lakers had several more games to play. There was still a chance he might be forced out into the open. Meanwhile there were some things I had to do.

For openers, I got into my heap and drove down to the water to find a boat.

The development planners of Marina Del Rey badly underestimated the vast numbers of nautical nuts waiting to play games with dinghies and davits. The dream of Venice had faded; the planned lagoons, canals and waterways missing their appointment with destiny had sunk into decay, rotting along with the rest of the waterfront town. Santa Monica, too, had passed along into its own faded history. Now along came Marina Del Rey, with its boat bait for swinging singles and wharf-hungry couples. In no time at all it had burgeoned into the fastest-growing play area on the West Coast.

Everybody wanted in on the action of the new nautical Suburbia West. Dockside supplanted patio action. They laid in streets with the names you associate with romantic adventuring in the South Seas.

There's Bali and Mindinao. Palawan and Panay. Bordering are the Marquesas, Tahiti, Fiji and Bora Bora.

Apartments shot up all around the man-made basin and beach. Liquor stores, picturesque restaurants and watering holes quickly followed. They had cute names like Pieces of Eight, the Captain's Wharf, the Admiral's Dinghy. They were jammed before the bar stools were firmly in place.

Then came the water play. Those who liked power in small gleaming hulled packaging bought their motorboats outright. Others rented them like cars. The ones with headier imaginations and more money to lay out went the windjamming route. They were skippers now, from the tiny cat-rigged skimmer sailboats to the big babies, the ornate, more prestige-pumping yachts.

The sloops and yawls and ketches ran with the wind in their own regattas. There were new commodores running the 2,225-mile race to Honolulu. The biggest apple of all was the Transpacific sea classic yacht race they could all dream of winning, the world's longest yacht race. It brought in the blue-water contenders who knew their way 3,571 miles right into Papeete harbor in time for Tahiti's Fete Nationale Week and Bastille Day celebration. The governor of French Polynesia was always available to present the racing trophies.

I parked my heap and found the man who ran slip rentals at Tahiti Marina, Marina Point and Pacific Harbor for Marina Del Rey. He didn't know of any Oriental owner or skipper.

The Small Craft Harbor Commissioner's office went through its ownership list and came up with a Lebanese and Tasmanian. The shaggy-haired whiz kid at UCLA who could beat the time of the voice-print computer had pronounced neither in the area of probables.

The man at the desk listened patiently as I vaguely put into words the meeting room on the boat I was seeking. It was the saloon, I learned. He also told me it sounded like no small craft to him, and had to come in at a quarter-ton or more, some of the racing yachts ranging up to ten meters. I had no idea if my mystery man raced his boat. He had other sporting ideas that interested me.

The harbor master checked his logging books, shook his head negative. No Chinese skipper, Burmese, Laotian or Thai. "It's quite possible the man you're looking for could be operating under another owner's registry papers."

The same thought had occurred to me. The harbor master said he would keep his eyes open for sinister-looking strangers and that meanwhile I was free to check the boats at the dock slips. I looked out his sun-splashed windows. Hundreds of various-sized craft were cluttering up the marine waters, their masts forming a spirelike network that seemed to extend to the horizon. I thanked him, gave him my card and left.

Panay Way had a down ramp leading to its boat slips. The slatted dock boards had been freshly hosed down by an early-rising environmentalist. Without rubber-soled boat shoes it was easy to get to the bottom dock walk fast.

I slid to the bottom, still erect. Anchored boats were gently bobbing on either side of me. Those in the immediate area were mostly small sail and power boats in the twenty-five-foot class. I was looking for bigger game and headed along the narrow dock walk toward the open water where the larger ones were moored.

There were all kinds, all sizes, jaunty, powerful and expensive-looking. The saloon to which I had been shanghaied might have been among them, but it would have taken a platoon of men to go through them all. I shook my head, gnashed my teeth and eyed them angrily, knowing the task was hopelessly out of my time schedule.

I lit a cigarette, rocked back on my heels and stared hard at them all, hoping for some clue and realizing there was none. I had been unconscious when brought here and my condition hadn't improved noticeably.

I heard voices and footsteps behind me on the upper walk. These were private dockings where I stood and I turned to retrace my steps. I flipped my butt into the water, watched it arc and hit, and looked up.

Three faces were looking expressionlessly down at me. Two of them were familiar. They were masks, of course, and one of them was a rube, the other a gorilla.

They turned as I hunched and started for them, and were running away from the railing before I had taken two steps. I ran along the narrow dock boards, hoping to cut them off, cursing the damp boards as I slithered and skidded almost out of control. I got to the inclined ramp, figuring my angle was good enough to cut them off, vaulted the iron railing, landed with my arms well extended on the other side, and swallowed hard.

Under the three masks were diminutive people. Kids.

"Gee, mister," piped the rube. "We didn't mean to scare you."

The gorilla head nodded in tandem. "These masks scare almost everybody."

All three heads came to about my belt line. The third one was new to me, and I wondered, with quickening pulse, if this was the way the sets ran when you checked them out.

I looked steely-eyed down at the skinny tyke. "Who are you supposed to be?"

His childish treble was indignant. "Wolfman! Who else?"

I shook the old head. No butterflies fell out. Pointing over the railing to the dock slips below, I said, "From down there you fellows looked awfully big. No wonder you scared me!"

They looked at one another, pleased.

"Yes, sir," I blabbered on, "those are great masks. I know a few people I'd like to scare, too. Remember where you bought them?"

The gorilla waved a thin arm to the north and west. "Lincoln," he said.

The rube shook his head negative. "Washington," he said firmly.

I looked down at Wolfman once more. "You decide."

"On the corner," he said, pointing toward the same area. "Lincoln and Washington. A little toy store. They got some great Draculas too. Only we liked these."

I lugged out three quarters. "Here," I told them. "Buy yourselves Dracula, too. Be my guests."

They shook their heads, I thought politely. When I brought my hand with the coins closer, Wolfman again solved the impasse. "Those are no good," he explained. "Draculas cost thirty-five cents each."

I added a dollar bill. "Live it up," I told them.

A little bell over the door tinkled a tinny alarm. The shopkeeper was old and had long ago given up looking happy to see a customer. He sat stonily behind his counter, waiting for me to sell him on what I wanted.

"You sell those Halloween masks?" I asked.

He waved a lethargic pale hand behind him. "All kinds we got. Staring you right in the face."

I followed his gesture to an upper shelf behind him. A solid line of masks was looking sightlessly down on me. I saw the three I was interested in. Gorilla, rube and wolfman. There were a few Draculas, too, and a Frankenstein monster, a bilious green.

I pointed to the trio on the left. "I just saw some kids at the marina wearing those three."

He nodded, unsmiling. "Business has been good lately. When I sell three more, maybe I can retire."

"A few days ago, maybe a week, some men could have been in here and bought three of them. Would you remember?"

He shrugged fragile shoulders. "What's to remember? People are in here all the time. You can see what a booming business I'm running here." He threw his hands apart to take in the deserted store. "They buy card tricks, leaking glasses, golf balls that explode. You want me to remember every customer?"

I took out a five-spot and placed it on the counter. "Not everybody. Just three men. I remember two masks they had. The rube and gorilla. I can't remember the third."

His hand was busy folding the bill. "What's to remember? The big fellow without the middle finger, he bought the wolf-man."

"How do you remember the middle finger when you're so busy here?" I asked.

He shrugged. The bill had disappeared. "When you try on a mask, you use your hands, no? So if a middle finger is missing, somebody would notice it, don't you think?"

I laid down a tenner. "I like your memory. What did the others look like?"

He stared down at the bill without moving. "This must be important to you," he said. "You could buy a lot of masks for that kind of money."

"I need the men more," I said. "They fooled me the other night. It's my turn to get even, but I want to be sure I pull the trick on the right fellows."

"I'll have to think about it," he said stolidly.

"Take your time. I wouldn't want to make a mistake."

He spat. "They were gunzels, no? Your friends?"

"Maybe," I said. "But not my friends."

His head cocked. "So what's to stop them from breaking me apart for being so nice to you?"

I indicated the ten-spot. "The sooner you remember, the sooner I can find them. When I find them, you won't have to worry."

He looked into my eyes, unconvinced. "All three of the hoodniks?"

I flipped my wallet open to show him the buzzer. "It's all in a day's work, pops. Try to remember."

He frowned and cast his eyes over my head toward the ceiling. "To begin with, they were all big, like yourself. The blond fellow—he took the farmer mask. That's all I remember for him. Light blond hair like straw. I suppose with the yokel mask, he felt at home."

That would be the rube. Lloyd.

"The fellow with the pockmarks on his face. That would be the gorilla. Dark—not black, you understand me. Dark skin, pockmarks. I think maybe even a scar on his face." He touched his own jaw on the left side and nodded, pleased. "Not the sort of man I'd want to do business with. He was maybe as big as you but wider." He lifted his shoulders and flexed his arms to widen his scrawny chest. "A real gorilla. If you ask me, he didn't need the mask."

"You don't remember any names?"

He shook his head. "They were laughing, not talking."

"I don't suppose they've been back in the neighborhood since?"

"To my knowledge, no—and I'm not complaining." He looked down at the tenner again. Surprisingly, he pushed it back toward me. "Frankly, it's worth ten dollars to me if you catch those no-goodniks, mister. You're a detective, no?"

"Yes, but we can't work without information." I pushed back the bill. "It's all yours."

"In that case," he said. He turned, surprising me with his agility, and handed me a mask off the line behind him. "Have one on the house."

"Is it my size?"

He shrugged. "Try it on. There's the mirror."

I tried it on. The mirror reflected the awesome green pallor of Frankenstein's monster. It was gratifying to know that just as the mystery man's hoods had picked masks that were extensions of their own personalities, I had attracted my own, in turn.

I put the mask in my pocket, hoping I'd have the chance to scare somebody with it soon.

"Thanks, pops. If this works, I'll be back for more."

"In that case," he said, "you better make sure you do a good job."

Eight

The neighborhood was dirty and run-down, but I didn't have to live in it. O. J. Burr had asked if I still had my connections. I was there to find out.

There were a lot of words on fences, the kind they don't allow on TV. There were gang slogans painted with thick brush strokes, covering anything available. Curses, threats, unsavory invitations to the fuzz. All in tne colorful argot of the street. Chicano talk. Black talk. Whitey talk.

The school fences were padlocked, strips of barbed wire across the top. The occasional window still lined with glass glittered next to those raped by rocks. The school grounds were concrete and deserted. If there were any living students about, it was a well-kept secret.

A beat-up green Corvair was parked near a fire plug. The driver slouched indolently on the worn leather, working a scratch sheet. I knew him as Benny the Runner. He was a street agent working for a local bookmaker. Benny covered policy action and any kind of betting action favored by the citizens. He had been around a long time, was honest and diligent, and could always be found parked in that same no-park ten-dollar zone. He had never been ticketed because the fuzz had their picks to back with a few bucks, too.

Every few minutes he had to drop his sheet and do a little roadside business through his window. Cars pulled up and double-parked beside him long enough to get down in Benny's book. The sidewalk action kept coming intermittently, and I watched from around the corner impatiently.

A few years back I had done Benny the small favor of his not being found floating face down in the Pacific. A couple of unprincipled mobsters had moved in on his action, siphoning off his numbers money. The tough men higher up that Benny ran for weren't interested in hard-luck stories. They understood only the daily take. I managed to outmuscle the hijacking hoods and brought back Benny's illicit loot. He swore up and down his wife and kids would always be grateful, as they hated to dress up for funerals. Now I waited for the street action to cool, to test his always fantastic memory for small favors, as well as bets and numbers.

The last happy spendthrift pulled away and I drove up alongside the paint-bleached green sedan. "Roper!" he said. "Jeez! Did I do somethin'?"

"I wouldn't know, Benny. I need some inside talk."

His eyes snapped back to the scratch sheet but his mouth was busy. "Around the corner on the right is a phone booth. Outside the laundry. Park the heap and dial a number. I can take a break here in a minute."

I followed the line, parked and picked up the idle phone. Benny wheeled around. Ignoring me, he went directly to the phone directories stacked on the outside wall. His face was carefully averted as he flipped over the yellow pages. "Okay, talk. Whaddaya need?"

"First, was there a scam on the Lakers?"

He wet his thumb, turning a page. "Jeez! I dunno. I ain't heard nothin'."

It's called a scam when a gambler gets to a player or team to shade some points, to manage to lose so he can win betting against the team. It's also called a fix, throwing it.

"Okay," I said into the dead phone, my eyes on Benny. "Who's been heavy on the action?"

I saw his tobacco-stained fingers tremble. The question wasn't a fair one. The ones who answer that kind live only long enough to regret it. "I won't push hard, Benny, but I have to know. Gonzaga was a friend of mine."

He flipped a few pages over, obviously paying no attention.

44

His fingers ran down a page and he tore it out. He came right for the phone booth I occupied and acted surprised to see it tenanted. "You gonna hog that box forever, Mac? Give somebody else a crack at it, huh?"

I hung up. He elbowed me aside impatiently as I stepped out. One hand was in his pocket, rummaging for coins. "Jules Belmont," he muttered from the side of his mouth. "You got it? Belmont. He's heavy." He dropped a coin into the box and pulled the folding door shut. He dialed and his eyes met mine for the first time.

I looked indignant. "Watch who you're pushing, you little jerk!"

"Up yours, Jack!"

From the Academy performance Benny was giving, there were eyes and ears and instant TV up and down the street. Looking mad, I stalked to my heap, fired it up and wheeled off. Benny was still playing his imaginary game, his back turned to me.

The harbor master came out of his office wearing a golf bag on his back. He didn't look happy to see me again.

"It won't take long. I've a name to check against your ownership list."

He dropped the bag, sighed and got out the door key. "What's the name?"

"It would be better if I just looked it over."

He found the registry book and opened it for me. I took it aside and flipped a few pages.

Belmont had a boat. *Dakar Doll.*

It stood at Slip 2204, Panay Way.

I closed the book and handed it back to the man. He heaved his golf bag back over his shoulder and got the door open.

As we walked out, I asked over my shoulder, "How big is the *Dakar Doll?*"

"Big enough," he said. "One-hundred-foot power yacht. Range of about fifteen hundred miles. Sleeps twelve. Party room for about fifty."

"Thanks," I said, starting away.

"If you're thinking of going aboard, better make it much later tonight."

"Any particular reason?"

"Belmont's armed guard might be asleep then."

I had time to iron out other details. The Forum front office told me the team hadn't left yet for New York and were working out at the local Loyola University gym. It was handy to the airport, and the university had made it easy for the Lakers to run their practice sessions there.

I could hear the whooping sounds and the lovely swishing the baskets made the moment I stepped out of my car. They weren't bothering with any security-guard detail and I walked right in the open gym door.

Laker coach Bryant was a stickler for team practice; his team was a running one, and even now, with a bare hour before boarding a plane, he had them digging and going through all the motions. I caught Bryant's eye, and he motioned his men to continue while he sauntered over. He was a big man, wearing a sweatsuit and perspiring as if he had been doing a lot of running.

Our acquaintance went back a few years to the time when he was a dangerous shooter for the Celtics. Never the team high-scorer, he had made the baskets when they were needed. His winning record had brought him to Los Angeles to add a little more fire to the talented but heretofore luckless Lakers. Buzz Bryant dipped into his personal bag of tricks and came up with the one ingredient the team needed—moxie. Heart. Bryant had so much of it, there was enough left over to equip the team right down to the secondaries.

"Another half-hour and you would have missed us," he said. "We're catching the next plane out."

"Who's taking over for Gonzaga?" I asked.

Bryant turned and indicated a broad-shouldered beanpole almost seven feet tall lazily floating through the air to stuff in a one-hander with nobody blocking him out.

"Ellis Decker," Bryant said. "Didn't get a chance to play much last year but he's got the moves."

46

"I'd like to talk to him, Buzz."

"Sure. Anything new?"

I shook the old head. "Going through the motions." I wagged my thumb at the yelling gang working the gym floor and couldn't keep the frostiness out of my voice. "Somebody might think they don't know Gonzaga's dead."

Bryant glared. "You ought to know better. It took me five hours to get them down here to work. They know what happened. They also know they're hired to win some more ball games."

The words were out and I didn't want them back. I didn't feel I owed him an apology either. "How many games do you have in New York?"

"Three."

"Any phone calls?"

Bryant blinked. Recovering, he scolded me with cold eyes. "Is that how it started with Gonzaga?"

"Started and finished," I said. "He wasn't listening when I told him he wasn't supposed to play."

"He never let on to me." Bryant scowled and looked down the polished gym floor at the lanky giants going through their moves. "Nobody on the team has mentioned anything. You think Decker is important enough for them to bother about? He's still a rookie, coming in with a cold hand."

"I don't know. Maybe he can convince me."

"I'll send him over." Bryant turned, whistle in hand. "You joining us in New York?"

I shrugged. "I might have to. Somebody's putting up a lot of juice and wouldn't like your team to win."

Bryant shook his head despondently. "Gamblers. Why the hell can't they stay out of it?" He knew there wasn't any answer and started away. "Try not to scare the kid. He'll be tight enough without it."

I waited for Decker to lope over. His lanky frame was deceptive and contained a lot of power. Not enough, however, to make up for the big man who had caught the four big bullets.

"I'm Ellis Decker," he said, extending a hand no bigger than a gravedigger's shovel. "I heard you were a friend of Gonzaga."

"Off and on," I said. "You may have heard why he was killed. Have you had any calls about shading points?"

"Who, me? Man, I'm nobody. Nobody heard of me."

"Maybe it's time they did. All you have to do is go out and play like Gonzaga."

He grinned. "That'll be the day. Ain't nobody living got his power. I'm okay, I guess, but I ain't never gonna beat Jo-Jo's time."

"Anyway, you'll have to try, won't you?"

"Sure, and maybe I'll get hot for the Knicks." His brown eyes rolled slyly. "Only one thing Jo-Jo did, maybe I could match him."

"What might that be?" I asked stodgily.

"His play with women," he said, laughing. "Especially that blond terror he been playing lately. Man, I'd sure like a piece of her action."

"Who's that?" I asked.

"That Joanna Burton gal. A real sweet-looking chick."

"What does she do?"

Decker blinked, surprised. "Don't you get around none? She sings at the Gin and Gaslight Club. Man, is she something else!"

"Did he see much of her?"

Decker snickered. "All he could get, is all. They been sweet and cozy a long time." He shook his head. "I never asked Jo-Jo no favors. Man, I sure wish now I'd asked him just the once for an introduction. I'm still nobody, see, but it don't mean it got to be always. Maybe if I make superstar, she might allow me some sweet talk. For that gal I could shoot me one hell of a lot of baskets."

I smiled. "She sounds like you'd find a lot of competition."

Reality took the smile off his face. "Man, don't I know it! Well, anyway—"

I shook his hand. "Good luck in New York. Maybe I'll look her up and tell her you think you're ready. If she's so nice, maybe she'll let you be a superstar on credit."

Decker grinned again. "Thanks, man. I'm ready now."

I watched his easy lope back to the other players, and walked out the gym door toward my parked heap. I didn't know about any blond terror's in Gonzaga's life. He was popular with the ladies, as he called them, and I had supposed he was playing the field. With his superstar status and life style, having a celebrity along with it was nothing exceptional. I could smile at her impact on young Decker. Gonzaga would have swept anything he fancied off a shelf and thought nothing of it.

Nine

The Gin and Gaslight Club was off Cienega on the Santa Monica strip. It featured rock-oriented, country-flavored romanticists. Troubadours and stylists like Kristofferson and Elton John, Jackson Browne and John Prine, charismatic singer-song-writers. These were all big names in the album field; I had been too busy to notice if Joanna Burton had cut anything.

She came on enormously sensual in a hot-red tank top shirt and tight black pants obviously glued to her buttocks. She sang six solo numbers with a small combo behind her, keyboard, bass and guitar. She radiated self-condfience, and along with it she was a visual and musical knockout. If she didn't screw up her career, it was apparent she was only a few more appearances from the standing-room-only crowd of the big-selling album people who had preceded her here.

I nursed a few drinks through her songs and handed a waiter a bill for his service along with a note for her.

The applause died rather quickly when she finished and a young man with long yellow hair and more than a decent amount of acne and pimples took her place on the floor. The audience let me know instantly this was what they had been waiting for. Burton, good as she was, still was secondary with this crowd. They were young ones mostly, and it was sad for an old campaigner to see pimples taking it over a well-formed and enticing keester. I didn't get his name because I got more pleasure watching the girl blonde walk toward me swinging her hips through the crowded tables on the floor.

Her stage smile was still fixed and she seemed a lot smaller offstage. She drummed the little piece of notepaper with her fingers as she sat down. I asked her what she was having, and it was a double bourbon.

"Max Roper?" she said, referring again to the note. "You sound familiar but I forget why. You're not an agent?"

"If I were, you'd get all my action. How well did you know Jo-Jo Gonzaga?"

She caught her breath and a trace of fear entered her deep blue eyes. "What's it to you? Who are you? Fuzz?"

"No." I explained my line. "Gonzaga was a friend. I've a pretty good idea who killed him and why. I could be wrong, and that's why I'd like to ask you a few questions."

She folded her arms and eyed me stonily. "If you know who killed him, why are you crapping around here? Did Jo-Jo tell you I was a good lay, or something?"

"Never mentioned it—good or bad." I waited till she had taken a good belt of her drink. "I'll have to assume it was good. I happen to know he was a busy man. He was troubled with insomnia but he knew ways to deal with it. If you were something special to him, I'm delighted."

She lit a cigarette. "Okay. So you're delighted. Now ask me what you want to know and make it fast." She wagged a thumb over her shoulder. "I'm due back on the stage with that jerk in a little while. We've got a duet to do. He's the main attraction here."

I shook my head. "They're making a big mistake. It should be you."

"Thanks a lot. It's Joe Coolidge they came to see. I'm only the warm-up." She reached across the table and patted my hand. "I'm sorry, I didn't mean to be nasty. This crowd makes me nervous. What do you want to know? If we don't have time for it all, we can finish at my place maybe Sunday. Here's the address." She scribbled quickly on the back of my note and handed it over.

"Sunday might be too late. First question, you weren't at Gonzaga's party the night he was killed. Any particular reason?"

She waved an expressive hand to take in the audience. "It's right here. You're looking at it. I work for a living."

"He was shot at four A.M. Were you working then?"

"I didn't know he was going to stop any bullets that night. Gonzaga finished his fun and games a lot earlier than I do. When I'm through here, sometimes I'm just beat. I took a rain check that night. I didn't have to answer to Jo-Jo for the times I couldn't make it. He was a reasonable man."

"If he was," I said, "I can't remember the last time. Maybe I've been missing something."

She smiled quickly and the lights went on again. "Oh, sure, I know what you mean. He was very impatient and got mad easy. But it was different with us."

I was about to ask her how different, but the audience was applauding the feature performer with the lank yellow hair and the music had stopped. Joanna Burton was pushing her chair away from the table. "Sorry, I've got to cut out now. Call me. I'll give you all the time you want."

"One second." My hand had her wrist as she started away. She looked up at me quickly, again showing the trace of fear. "Just a quick one, Miss Burton. Did Gonzaga tell you he was going to be killed if he played the play-off games?"

Her eyes widened. "Jesus! You mean, he knew?"

I released her wrist. "Okay. Back to work. I'll call you."

She bobbed her blond head and wiggled her way back to the floor to join the pimpled idol still taking bows while waiting for her. Her voice followed me to the outer door: "It doesn't matter any more/ Who's right or wrong/ We've been lovers much too long/ Making believe is a wasting lie/ Each time we try it lately/ I want to die . . ."

The song reminded me I had forgotten my promise to Decker, to put in a good word for him. It would have to wait now.

I saw her again, framed in the spotlight when I left, a beautiful talented thrush with the kind of physical equipment that could disturb men. To be Gonzaga's favorite, she would have had to be something special, in the sack or out. The big man always had his pick of choice women, taking that aspect of his life as seriously as he took food and the court game that had made him famous. He prided himself on his collection of beautiful ladies just as he did on his prowess with a basketball. And he was a scoring machine in either field.

The particular delicate scent of Joanna Burton was still with me as I hit the damp night air. It lingered in my nostrils, trying to tell me something. There were many ways a man could die. The sweeter sex had provided some of them long before the game of basketball was invented.

Ten

At midnight the sky was overcast, fog drifting in. There were still merrymakers and revelers aboard some of the marina boats. I had marked Belmont's *Dakar Doll* at the far end and saw no lights. I sat in my car awhile longer on the upper drive waiting for the yellow blanket of fog to provide a little more cover.

A small party of loaded citizens came shuffling up the dockwalk, singing. Cars in the parking lot revved up and spun out. Boat lights went out. I went through the slip gate and down the wet ramp. Music sounded softly from some of the small boats gently moving on either side of the narrow walk as I made my way to the far end. There were regular boat dwellers here, insomniacs as well as romanticists.

The *Dakar Doll* was shrouded in the fog. Somewhere on deck a match scratched and briefly sputtered, its flare illuminating a man's face. He lit his cigarette, puffed, and disappeared in the mist.

I waited below in the deeper shadows for Belmont's guard to tell me where he was. He didn't, and I got tired of waiting around shivering in the cold night wind.

I swung up on the starboard side and groped forward through the mist. I sensed a movement a few steps ahead, heard a muttered curse, and froze. He puffed his cigarette, and I inched closer and made out the guard, his back to me. He was leaning against a spar.

"Goddamn," he said in a lighter vein. "Lousy no-good beer cans!"

The easy patented rip-off top had fouled and he worked over it, damning the can, its inventor and manufacturer. He jerked at it and the key tore loose in his fingers. I had empathy for his exasperation, but when he reared back to toss the offending can into the water, I stepped in and sapped him behind the ear with my gun, taking no chances with a mistimed karate chop. He went down with the merest grunt.

My pencil flash showed he wasn't any of the hoods I wanted. I left him out cold and found the cabin doorway. I stepped down into darkness relieved by windows on the aft side. My torch stabbed around and showed me a large sitting room, well appointed and carpeted. Big enough to hold a large party or conduct a business meeting.

The walls were paneled with good expensive wood, covered at intervals by paintings. There was a large desk across the room, a lamp covering one corner, a leather-topped executive chair behind. There were stuffed chairs, a sofa and a hard chair. I sat on the hard chair across the room from the desk, put my arms behind me and leaned back tautly. My nose did its job first, identifying the sea smell. I heard gulls but it still didn't prove anything.

Camino's forensic expert Doc Shipman had let me smell a sample of the drug similar to one they had used on me. The scent of the sea was stronger now but I needed more. I tried to remember.

My flashback mechanism had my wrists lashed together, arms tight behind me pressed to the hard chair-back. The man with the gorilla mask blocked my left side. Rube was to my right. The blinding light had stabbed suddenly out of the darkness, and the man behind it in the shadow was talking. I heard the same singsong words: "Gonzaga, I want Gonzaga."

He had told me what he wanted, I answered, and the man in the gorilla mask belted me backhand across the chops. The rube on my right made the floorboards creak as he leaned in for his own cheap shot. I remembered spitting my blood over his shoe, making him step back. "No, Lloyd," the man across the room had said.

I put my torch to work on the carpet, searching for bloodstains. Blood was still pretty good evidence, and Doc Shipman would tell me if I was crazy or not. If it was my own, I wanted to know it. My light held on a small discolored patch. I put it down, scraped at the rug fibers with my penknife. When I had enough, I carefully inserted the scraped threads and hairs in my notebook.

It was going inside my pocket when the floor creaked. The swift rustling movement behind me was faster than my reflexes and something hard and heavy knocked off the back of my head.

It wasn't any worse than being kicked by a horse. An interior dam between my ears exploded. Fiery rockets made strange swooshing sounds in erratic arcs behind my eyes. There wasn't too much distance between me and the floor and I made it easily, knowing I had just been murdered.

Secret agent had again been found out, and found wanting. The harbor master had slipped me an exclusive, that Belmont had a hired guard. I had forgotten to take into account the not too extravagant assumption that a wealthy big-time gambler like Jules Belmont could afford two.

I awoke briefly to the nasty sensation of choking in water. Making swimming motions seemed to make the feeling go away. After a while it got to be too much trouble. I went back to choking and sputtering. My lungs were trying to tell me we were in big trouble but my brain had already spread the news we were dead. A little isolated spark of instinct somewhere began to argue the point. I made more swimming motions.

My head made contact with another substance that was surprisingly equally solid. I forgot how to swim and went back to drowning. Then something seemed to lift me up by the hair. There was still a lot of water remaining to choke and retch with but somehow not as much as before.

I was lying on my back, staring straight up at a ceiling. The ceiling moved. I blinked, and when I opened my eyes there was a girl's face. It was fragmented, a prism face. Girls' faces have always interested me more than ceilings and I tried to concentrate on this one so I could remember where I had seen it before.

Her lips moved and formed words. "Don't tell me you're alive!"

I made up my own words to answer that. Nothing happened, unless retching counts.

She helped me sit up and get it out of my system. She held the basin under my chin until I was finished. "That's pretty awful stuff to have been drinking," she said. "Couldn't you find any bar open?"

I lay back and watched her, too tired and hurting to join in on the comedy hour. I thought of Tarzan. It was very clear to me that when he said "Me Tarzan, you Jane," he had been recently conked over the noggin and then tossed into the drink. From my viewpoint, he was overly talkative and demonstrative.

The ceiling behind the girl's head moved again. I became aware of other moving, rustling sounds. Dishes in transit. A chair going into its own orbit. Something groaned under my feet and spared me the trouble. My reliable smeller came up with more information.

"Are we on a boat?" I asked.

She clapped her hands, her mouth curiously joyful. "I'm glad you said that. I was beginning to think we were a funeral barge."

I reached for the back of my head. It was still there. My hand felt clammy and wet, but no wetter than the rest of me. "Somebody zonked me a good one," I said.

"I think you were also let out to drown," she said. "At least, that's what you seemed to be doing when I noticed."

My true noble spirit asserted itself. "My own fault. I got careless."

"It's all right," she said. "I wasn't doing much anyway."

Some of the cobwebs dissolved in my head. My vision cleared and I noted that without the fragmentation this girl's face was even prettier than before. "Is this your boat?"

She nodded. "I thought we already did that. This is my boat, my home and my castle. You're awfully damp. Would you like some brandy?"

"Try me."

She stepped away from me, turning her back, and reached up for a bottle alone on a recessed shelf. She was wearing pants and a loose sweater, but that didn't stop her from looking terrific. She came back with a glass for the bottle and she looked every bit as good front view.

"I don't know if this is good brandy. But then again, I don't even know if you're worth it," she said.

"Nobody's worth good brandy," I said.

It wasn't Napoleon's best year but it did the job. I felt better and tried sitting up on the narrow bunk. She put a firm restraining hand on my chest. "Better not, Mr. Roper. You may be seriously injured."

I started to shake my head, and stopped before it fell off. "How do you know my name?"

She showed me my wallet in her hand. "When I pulled you out, I thought you were dead. Seriously. I went through your pockets to find out who you were in case I—" She dropped it on my chest. "Well, anyway, you aren't."

"No," I said. "It only feels like it."

"What happened?"

"I got zonked. After that, I don't remember a thing." She looked too delicate to have hauled a heavy soaking stiff like me in. "How did you get me in here?"

"I was on deck having a final smoke. Something bumped my boat. I looked over the side and there you were. I'm stronger than I look."

"Thanks," I said. "Keep in shape. It helps."

"You keep saying you were zonked. What does *that* mean? Who are you, anyway?"

"A very dumb private eye."

"No kidding?" she said. "You mean like in the old B flicks on TV? Like Humphrey Bogart?"

"Bogart may have been a little better at it," I conceded. "But then again, I'm for real."

"I don't believe it," she said.

"I got my head bashed a while ago. That's zonking. I was thrown off somebody's boat and supposed to drown. That's for real, too."

"Why?"

I could still shrug my shoulders. "It's part of the deal."

"My God!" She stared, unbelieving. "A private eye in today's world? With all that's going on, and you're on some secret caper and get your head bashed nearly in? For a client, I guess?" I nodded, and she shook her head incredulously again. "Don't you see you're an anachronism? You're archaic."

"I know," I said. "But I'm too old for hijacking planes. How else in life could I find excitement?"

She pushed back her hair without wincing and I envied her sound scalp. "There's no need in today's world for knights in shining armor."

I touched my head gingerly. It was all there, only hurting. "You're right," I said. "But I think I'm in too deep to stop. I keep going on helping the weak and tired, the poor and helpless. Without me in there, slugging and doing good, it would all be chaos." A glance at my watch told me it was long past midnight. I sat up, feeling rotten. My feet were cold and soggy. "Thanks again for hauling me in. I'd better be going."

"You can't deceive yourself forever wearing a mask," she said. "You've got to find and come to grips with the awareness of the real you."

I looked at her hard, and she wasn't putting me on. I took another look at my watch and relaxed. There wasn't any place left to go but home, and that wasn't too much. I settled back, curled my toes and noticed idly they weren't wearing shoes.

"Okay," I said. "What are you selling?"

"I AM-ness," she said.

I shifted my eyes and didn't see my shoes anywhere. "What does it do?"

"The general principle is nonattachment. To un-become what I am not. Obviously, you weren't born to be a private eye, and you certainly won't be one forever. It doesn't make sense to identify with something in you that can change."

I stared curiously at my wet socks again. "I'm not arguing with what you're saying," I said. I lifted my feet. "I've been hit over the head before, but never hard enough to lose my shoes."

"Oh," she said, smiling, "the zonking didn't do that. I did." She swooped gracefully and picked some shoes up from behind her chair. "They were awfully wet." She turned them over and water dripped out. "They still are. Must you wear them now?"

"One pair at a time is all they issue us at Private Eye School."

She handed them over, and they were very wet. So were the laces, and they were tied and the bows had become knots. Knots in wet laces are a bummer. She must have noticed my unhappy look. "Sorry about that," she said. "I had to get them off any way I could."

"It's okay," I said, lying a little.

She watched me struggle awhile. "Don't get mad. Try to remember I saved your life . . . I think."

The latent cunning I had neglected to use on Belmont's boat was brought into play. I got the knots untied and back into neat little bows faster than any five-year-old. I stood up, hearing her cry too late, "Watch your head!"

I sat on her narrow bunk again, wondering if the principle of nonattachment covered feeling a kind of pride in the world's best going headache.

"I guess you're not used to boats," the girl was saying. "This one is very small. Only a seventeen-footer."

"It doesn't matter about size," I said, peaceful and resigned. "Belmont's is a lot bigger and I hurt my head there, too."

"Belmont's?"

"The *Dakar Doll*. The big baby at the end of the dock."

She was shaking her head, making it look easy. "There's nothing like that here."

I put the steely glint back in my eye. "Isn't this the Panay Way boat slip?"

"No." She pointed over my right shoulder. "This is Palawan. Panay's across there. You must have drifted a lot. No wonder you were so wet."

I thought about it and couldn't remember swimming.

The girl was up, making sounds at a cupboard. "I'll put up some tea. Are you going back to that other boat to get yourself zonked again?"

"Not tonight. I'll take the tea. It's probably safer."

She brought it back, scented and steaming hot, and let me kill some more of her brandy. "That's very good," she said, "about your not going back there. That's real I AM-ness."

"I never thought I'd make it," I said. "How did I do it?"

"By renouncing the object of the ego's craving," she said. "You want to go back because your pride is hurt, but you decided not to."

"You're right. My head hurts worse than my pride."

The overhead lamp of the cabin swayed gently. The girl sat gracefully at the table, feet tucked under her. "Is this case so private you can't discuss it?"

"A friend of mine was killed."

Her head sank forward. A slim sunned hand played with her long black hair. "I'm sorry. I guess that's what you have to expect when you discuss something with a dumb hippie-type girl."

"You saved my life tonight. So far I haven't begun to notice how dumb you are. Also, you know my name and I don't know yours."

"Barbara."

"Okay, Barbara. What's the rest of the handle?"

"You won't like it," she said.

I grinned. "Try me. I'll try not to laugh."

"Belmont," she said softly.

I rubbed my jaw. It ached. "I give up," I said finally. "What's the connection?"

"Jules Belmont is my uncle."

Eleven

It was close to three in the morning when I pulled in to the parking stall in the rear of my apartment building. The fog had cleared, the moon riding pale and high in a star-cluttered sky over Santa Monica. Ordinarily I would have thought it beautiful, but the untoward events of the night had ruined not only my head, suit and lungs, but my disposition.

After having bungled my midnight foray to the *Dakar Doll*, I hadn't bothered with a return trip. Although I had made it a fiasco, I felt reasonably sure in my mind that it was indeed the boat where the mystery man had me brought, slugged, drugged and given the order for Gonzaga not to play.

Water Baby was the given name for Barbara Belmont's little boat. I had left it reluctantly, without dipping into any of the details with the I AM-ness girl concerning her Uncle Jules. She wouldn't have known what I was talking about, certainly not believed any part of it. She knew a lot about him, but nothing about the part of his life that interested me.

Apparently she was the poor relation. "He's one of the filthy rich," she told me, following her initial revelation. "All the oil wells in Texas, or practically. That's helped build his art collection. It may go to a museum some day; worth a few million, I heard. Then, he has that chain of restaurants all over the West Coast. Gentleman Jim's. Only another fortune there." She sighed, smiled, and poured more tea from an antique samovar. "Uncle Jules has the Midas touch. Everything he handles turns into gold. I hardly ever see him."

"You park your boats in the same marina," I pointed out.

Her dark eyes flashed. "He doesn't own everything. I pay for my docking. That may be the only thing we have in common—we both like to be in the water."

I didn't want to break the news that her uncle might be in different water, deeper and more tepid. She got around to part of it on her own after a while. "What were you doing on board the *Dakar Doll* tonight, anyway?"

I made it brief. "Business call."

She nodded, smiling, having it all in her head after so many of the Bogarts and B flicks. "I know. You probably did a job for Uncle and asked for a lot of money. I could have told you he's awfully cheap. He'd probably sooner have a man knocked over the head than pay a bill when it's due."

"I know now," I said. "Next time I'll bill him through the mail."

"That's a better way, I think. He's one of those types who hates being stampeded, wants things his own way. He had to fight for everything he got on the way up, you know, and now he hates to give any part of it away. That museum collection of his, for example. He promised it to them years ago. But he still holds on to it. I don't even know if he appreciates art, or for that matter, artists. He knows that I paint, for instance. But he never yet offered to buy anything. Not that I'd sell him the smallest picture," she added firmly. "He won't even look."

"What do you paint?"

"People," she said. "Things."

"I'd like to see some of them."

She shook her head, the long hair tossing gently with it. "Not tonight."

I asked her why not tonight, and she told me, "Your eyes aren't in focus."

"Okay. Maybe we can make it some other time when my head is better."

"Fine," she said. Then, shyly, "You don't even have to leave tonight, if you don't feel like it. I mean, I've an extra bunk over there. This boat sleeps two."

I looked at her with the off-focus eyes and made out a blush. "I'd like to," I said. "But I better go home."

"Anybody waiting for you there?"

"Nobody."

She smiled. "Wonderful," she said. "Maybe I'll get you yet."

"I'm a pushover. How old are you?"

"Nineteen. Well, almost."

I got up, watching my head. "I'm leaving."

"What's wrong with nineteen?" she asked. "I've got all my own teeth."

"Nineteen is beautiful," I said. "How do you get off this ship?"

"It's not a ship, it's a boat. And you're chicken."

"Which way out?"

She stood up, slim and gracefully formed. "The same way you came in. Only you wouldn't remember."

She helped me off and turned it somehow into a gentle but warming goodnight kiss. "Hey, that's great," she said after a second.

"I thought so too," I said.

"I mean, that put your eyes back in focus."

I got her reluctantly out of my mind on the drive home. I stayed with Uncle Jules. Benny the Runner had him down as a heavy bettor. It didn't make any difference that Belmont was legitimate, a nonprofessional gambler. The rich have gambling fever too. Unlike the rest of the poor suckers, they can afford to go heavy on the action. Bet big. If they lose, they have more where that came from.

Some of the big men don't like losing. Being successful, they have the winning habit. They like to keep it that way. Remembering what his niece had told me about his penurious ways, I put another mental check against Belmont. How far would a man go who hates to lose, hates paying off?

If Benny the Runner knew Belmont was betting heavy on the games, others would know. Unlike most big cities, Los Angeles is a peculiar gambling town in that it has no big crime kingpin, no organized syndicate. Chief Parker had seen to that when he started his clean-up drives, and subsequent law officers had made it stick. The small operators were tolerated, the five-and-dime bookmakers. Independents who wheeled and dealed and handled the action without getting big enough to threaten anybody or control anything. There were roughly thirty-five gambling spots. The annual take was estimated at close to a billion dollars. All spread out, some for everybody. The fuzz had found policy tapes in an old lady's shopping bag. It revealed a $580,000 operation.

Belmont, like any really big gambler, could have been laying off all over town. Vegas would take his money too, although it was considered dangerous to use the phones. Still, whoever wanted to get burned badly enough could always find the way.

Smart money laid the odds and the bookmakers figured the point spreads they would allow and marked their sheets accordingly. They met once a week to settle with their clients afterward. Everybody made good his bet. Otherwise you couldn't play the game.

Scamming was murder for a professional gambler and would have been equally disastrous for a legit businessman like Belmont. Perhaps he had bet so heavily that he thought to protect his interest. But I couldn't prove it. No more than I could prove the carpet fibers with the curious bleached-out stain contained detectable elements of my blood. They had been washed out of my pocket along with my case.

Yet I remained dead certain the boat was his, the same boat I had been brought to, the order coming from the singsong man in the shadows behind the light. The singsong man could be the front man for the Asian drug exporters. I couldn't prove that either. I didn't know his name or if he was waiting around for me to find him. Trying to link Belmont with this narcotic lead seemed ridiculous. As the hippie-type niece had said when I owned up to being a private eye, "I don't believe it." I couldn't believe, either, what I had on Belmont. I was working the wrong side of the street. I had to be in error somewhere.

Some straight judicious thinking was indicated. Also some booze, a hot shower and some sack time. Any or all of these, I thought, might put me on the right track. I got started up the stairs to my apartment, wet shoes squishing, clothes heavy and sodden, weary and confused.

I didn't open my door right away because a man was down, lying in front of it. He was long and lanky, he had red hair and a lot of blood on his face. He looked dead but he wasn't.

He groaned when I turned him over. We hadn't been that chummy, but I knew him. It was Tom Power, the former Laker shooter, current Forum security guard. We hadn't met or spoken since Gonzaga was knocked off on his balcony.

I shook him awake. His pale-blue eyes blinked and stared at me without comprehension. "Power, what the hell happened?"

His long angular jaw gaped. "Jesus, Roper, are you still living? I thought they got to you too."

Even the boniest of the six-fours aren't lightweight. I got him off the floor and hauled him inside. I dumped him into a soft chair, broke out the booze and ice and splashed some into large glasses for us. "Who's they? What are you talking about?"

He gulped a mouthful first and wiped his mouth with the back of his hand. "You know. Those three guys you told me about. The ones you said were after Gonzaga. I came over to talk to you. They jumped me as soon as I got out of the car. They belted me around and told me you'd get more of the same if you didn't lay off."

I was puzzled. "Why did they slug you? They don't know you." Another thing I hadn't figured out yet was how the hoods knew me well enough to pick me up at my pad. There was no way they could have figured Power was connected, unless they had spotted me talking to him in the Forum parking lot.

"I dunno," Power said. "Maybe they think because I know you, I'm entitled to get my licks." He looked sideways at me. "I guess you didn't tell anybody, huh, I was helping you and Jo-Jo?"

"Don't be an ass. What the hell kind of help did you do? You're supposed to be a security guard. You were just doing what your job calls for in the Forum."

He downed another slug. "Yeah. I guess."

"What did they look like?"

He put a hand to his head, trying to remember. It came away with a thin bloody film. Power stared at it, his hand shaking. He turned his head to me, waving his bloody hand in helpless motions. "I wish to hell I could tell you. But I guess they were the same three guys—"

"Three? Are you sure?"

He paled and swallowed hard. "Well, I thought it was three. You said three, didn't you? They were big. I know that. You called that right. Only you didn't mention how hard they hit." He rubbed a swelling purpling bruise on his right cheekbone.

There wasn't a chance they had mistaken Power for me, if it was the same three hoods. "Were they wearing masks?"

"What? Masks? I dunno. It was dark in the alley. I got hit from behind. On my way down, they belted me some more in the ribs. I'm pretty sure there were three of them. At least! About the masks, when I hit the ground, I figured it made sense to just lay there, like pretending I was out. I didn't bother looking. That's when they started talking. About you getting more of the same if you don't lay off."

"Lay off what? Did they say?"

"I got the idea they meant your investigation. You're going after them for knocking off Gonzaga, aren't you?"

"Right. Did they say anything else?"

"No, but they'd made their point, far as I was concerned. I just laid there, playing possum. I didn't go after them. I'm no pro like you. I'm no goddamn hero, Roper."

I splashed more booze into his glass. "Nobody's expecting it of you. I never thought you'd be brought into it, Power. I'm sorry. What did you want to see me about tonight?"

He pulled the glass off his lip. "What?"

"You said you came over to talk to me. What about?"

He studied his glass sullenly. "Oh, yeah, that. Well, first I wondered how you were doing catching those guys who knocked Gonzaga off. I guess it ain't easy catching up to them, so I wanted you to know I'm willing to help. Any way at all."

"Thanks, but I usually work alone. Anything else?"

"Yeah. I didn't know if you knew Decker was replacing

Gonzaga. He's still wet behind the ears. So I wondered if you were going to look after him now. And the same deal—if I can help. Hell, the Lakers are still my old team."

"Help with Decker? How?"

"I don't know," Power said glumly. "But there oughtta be some way. The kid's all jazzed up now, he can't wait to go places. Don't forget, I still hang around with the guys a lot. Decker's lived in Gonzaga's shadow for so long, he's got his future all planned. Says he's gonna start right where Gonzaga left off with the ladies. There's a cute blond singer at the Gin and Gaslight Club, Joanna Burton. She was Jo-Jo's chick, but Decker isn't going to let that stop him. He's set to move right in there."

I smiled. "Oh, so he told you that, too."

"Yeah," Power said. "I'm just a sort of old father confessor type to him and the other guys. What the hell can I do but listen?"

"Maybe he's ready now," I said. "Maybe he doesn't need help. Why would anybody want to rub him out?"

"How the hell would I know?" Power said, ruffled. "You say he don't need any help, that's fine with me. But I got that big .38 I use at the Forum for guard duty. Believe it or not, in the war I was pretty good with a gun. Got me a lot of hits." He yanked his trouser up the gimpy leg. "The knee's bad but I can still move around with this steel support brace." He dropped the cloth and slapped his knee, grinning wildly. "Yeah, Decker's a swinger, but that cat's got a lot to learn if he thinks he can match Gonzaga's time." He shook his head. "No way."

"That's what I thought. But who knows? Maybe he has the incentive now."

Power smirked. "Incentive, hell. Like I said, he's wet behind the ears. But if anybody's out to get him, I wanna help."

Power surprised me. In my book, he was a cold duck, withdrawn, nursing his private grudge against the world. "You've got a family, haven't you?" I asked.

"A wife and a couple of wise-guy kids," he snapped. "So what? I'm my own boss. It's got nothing to do with them."

I leaned to take a closer look at his bruised face. "You caught a good one. You okay to drive home?"

"Are you kidding? Sure I'm okay. I been slugged before—guys bigger than these hoods. I played pro ball a lot of years. What do I look like—some kind of pantywaist?"

"I didn't mean it that way," I said. "If you're all right, fine. I had a rough night myself. I'm beat, it's late and I want to hit the sack. Thanks again for coming over, and I'm sorry you were hurt. It's supposed to be my line, not yours."

Twelve

In my dream, I knew I had the killer. He was tall and red-haired, he walked with a limp, he spoke in a singsong Chinese patois, and he lived wildly on a hundred-foot yacht in the marina with willing beauties in every stateroom. The middle finger of his left hand was missing, he had a huge Great Dane guarding him, and he answered to the name of Little Benny, the Runner. I had him run down in a garish night club lit by gaslight and pinned to the wall, when my phone rang and I let him get away.

I recognized the nasal disapproving voice instantly, knew my killer was a fraud, anyway, and shook the remaining fog out of my head. "This is Dr. La Salle," he said. "UCLA. Is this Roper?"

"Yes. What can I do for you, Doc?"

"You can keep your damn cheap little private-eye capers out of this office in the future, for one thing. We're not here to service your kind of shoddy operation."

"Fine," I said pleasantly. "I'll mention that to the people who allowed you the grant to work out the bugs in your computer at public expense. Anything else?"

He was silent for a moment, and I pictured him beetle-browed and pouting. "Don't be such a goddamn smart-ass," he said. "You know why I'm calling."

"You just told me, didn't you? You didn't want to service my kind of shoddy operation. You did say *shoddy?*"

"Whatever I said, goes. Apparently you are so busy being a

great private detective, you're not aware when you are being followed. Do you understand now what I'm talking about?"

"Not yet, Doc, but keep at it. Maybe it will come."

"I'm telling you," he yelled, "somebody broke into this office during the night and stole that tape you left. The one Miss Shaw was foolish enough to have worked on for you."

I sat up straighter. "Was Miss Shaw hurt?"

"No, she wasn't. No thanks to you. I said it was stolen during the night, remember? Miss Shaw works days."

"I'm really sorry to hear it," I said. "How did they break in, through the window?"

"How would I know," he said smugly, "I'm no detective. Maybe it was the window. Maybe it was the door. All I know is, it's disappeared. We're not used to that sort of thing around here—people, hoodlums breaking in."

I lit a cigarette to help me get started coughing earlier in the morning. "Is it possible you're mistaken? Perhaps Miss Shaw mislaid the tape."

"Listen, smart-ass," he said, "she didn't mislay anything. I happened to have gone over it last and I left it in plain view on my desk. Do you have any other bright ideas?"

He wouldn't have liked the only one I had. "I'll call Lieutenant Camino of Homicide and let him handle it. He'll send a crew of experts over there to check the premises for finger-prints. They'll be able to tell if the dude came in through the door or window."

La Salle frowned over the phone. "That's all we need. The police."

"They're always available to protect all us property owners. I suggest you don't touch anything meanwhile. You wouldn't want to blur any possible prints."

La Salle found a hidden reserve of irritation for his tone. "Don't tell me what I should or should not do in my own office. We've work to do here. I'm not responsible for your careless-ness, allowing your suspect to tail you here. That *is* the correct phrase, isn't it?" he added sarcastically.

"It covers it," I said. "But it's not necessarily true, La Salle, merely your assumption."

"Really?"

"The tape could have been taken for a variety of reasons, none of them related to this particular case. It could have been taken by one of your students, the cleaning woman, anybody. It might have fallen off your desk into the wastebasket and been disposed of that way."

"Nice try, Roper," he said, "but I'm not impressed with your theorizing. There hasn't been a single instance before of any missing tape since I've been here. Doesn't that suggest anything to you?"

"Offhand, that you're not as lucky as you used to be."

La Salle snickered. "Very funny. Perhaps instead of giving me smart-ass answers, you'd do better considering who knew you were coming here with that tape, and why."

I had already gone over that in my mind, covered half the world, and found them all singularly guiltless.

La Salle wasn't at such a loss with ready conclusions. "As a matter of fact," he was saying, "I can't understand why whoever took it waited until last night to break in. He could have come in after you left, stuck a gun in our faces, and walked right off with the tape in broad daylight."

"I agree with you there," I said.

"What?"

"The spool wasn't marked. How would anybody breaking in at night know what tape to look for?"

"Yes," La Salle said. "Curious, isn't it? But then, inasmuch as you are the detective, that's your problem, isn't it? Given sufficient time and a few unrelated and coincidental facts, I'm sure you will deduce just how he did it."

"Maybe," I said. "I don't know what's eating you about private investigators, La Salle. That's your hang-up. But there's another possibility I have to consider."

"Do tell," he said. "Is this one off the top of your head, too?"

"This one is easy. You got rid of the tape yourself."

There was a moment of silence, but it was too good to last. "Really? How impressive! Now why would I want to do that?"

"Several reasons. One, you didn't want to be bothered with the voice print from the beginning. Maybe you don't like the responsibility of becoming involved in a murder case. The tape was possible evidence against a killer."

"So you say," he said, scoffing, "but then, I don't take much stock in that, do I?"

"Second," I continued, "you don't like the idea of your Miss Shaw getting the attention and notoriety she might get if she was proven correct, beating your own computer to the analysis. It makes some kind of lopsided sense, then, for you to destroy the evidence, and pretend it was stolen. The story of the tape theft could be fabricated, you see."

While he thought about it, I got another butt going. When he got back on, his voice had a lot more ice in it. "If Miss Shaw happens to miss any possible attention and notoriety, as you suggest, and by my own doing, she might prove to be most grateful. You see, I've gone over that tape myself. It might surprise you to learn that I found Miss Shaw in error."

"Nothing surprises me, La Salle, I'm too old. In error, where?"

He registered a mock heavy surprise. "Don't tell me you really want to know?"

"Not too much. I think she knows her stuff. I'm willing to buy it. If you say she's wrong, go ahead. Lay it on me."

The shaggy-haired Miss Shaw had acknowledged La Salle's prowess in the field. He was the pioneer, good at the mechanical aspects, she the more intuitive. La Salle would have his own reasons for not going along, but I had to listen.

"Miss Shaw said Yunnan Province, China. South China. I would say the subject came from much farther north—Hopei Province. North China."

"Near Peking? You're saying Red China?"

"Precisely."

"Maybe you're wrong. Your computer card agreed with your assistant. It read: South China, Laos, Burma, Thailand."

"Computers can be wrong," he snapped.

"Sure," I said. "But it's your baby."

"Nevertheless," La Salle said stiffly, "the computer was in error. As was Miss Shaw."

"No indication of Laos, Burma or Thailand?"

"Very slight," he said. "The subject has a minor speech impairment. Enough to have induced Miss Shaw as well as the computer into error. It takes a well-trained ear to make adjustments and allowances for these particular nuances."

"Okay. Have you convinced Miss Shaw she was in error?"

"Not yet," he said. "But that is not surprising. Miss Shaw is well trained but she happens to be a stubborn person."

I woke Camino up to acquaint him with the latest scoop.

"That's a helluva thing to wake up a sleeping cop for," he said. "My job is homicide."

"That's why I called you first. I might just kill La Salle."

"Go ahead," Camino said. "I never did like the snotty sonofabitch."

"While we're in agreement, there's something else, Nick." I repeated the conclusions the whiz kid at UCLA had come to on the tape. "If she's right, my mystery man could be running a big heroin deal from Asia."

"I've got to be dreaming," Camino said, "or did somebody wake me up?"

"Our narc man Smith gave me the facts and figures. The big man there in northern Burma is Lo Hsinghan. My caller could be dropping it in from Mex."

Camino started coughing, and I knew it wasn't from chewing gum. "I'm Homicide," he said when his lungs permitted. "You want to talk about running dope, I'll give you a number."

"I've given you the dope talk. Now I want to tell you about Jules Belmont."

Camino listened to it all without laughing once. "They ought to give me a ribbon for this," he said at last. "This multimillionaire Belmont, you say? The one with the oil digs and art collection, the chicken and fish and chip franchises, the chain of restaurants, the newspaper and TV stations and cattle ranches, bet a bundle, you said?"

"The kid lied to me," I said. "All she mentioned was the oil wells, art collection and the Gentleman Jims."

"Maybe you were still unconscious, amigo, and didn't hear

it all. What I'm trying to get across is simple enough. Even if the guy stood to lose a fortune on the games, what can he lose? He's got a few other fortunes, right?"

"Right," I said, "but—"

"You want me to think he panicked and got Gonzaga knocked off for disobeying orders? Sounds screwy, but okay—I'll buy it. The guy's probably a megalomaniac, like the rest of them, when he says he wants something done, he means it. He could have knocked you off as well as Gonzaga, but Gonzaga was a superstar, and you ain't. You're not worth the trouble. If he's going to risk a murder rap, it's got to be for somebody important, right?"

"Now, listen—"

"I listened. Okay. Belmont knocks off Gonzaga for his own mysterious reasons. I like that. Why? Because it's so goddamn stupid, that's why. But now you want to tie him up with some runner from Asia pushing dope? Loaning him his boat for the deal with you so you can sniff around later, smell it out and pin it all on him? Is this what you want me to believe?"

"Now that you mention it," I said. "It does sound a little too much. I can't believe it myself."

"Okay. Anything else—that I can take seriously?"

"Not a thing."

"I suppose all that lovely evidence you scraped off the *Dakar Doll* rug washed away when they dumped you?"

"Right. I'm all that's left."

"Too bad," Camino said. "Doc Shipman deserves a good laugh now and then. Now he won't get the chance."

"I think I know where I made my mistake," I said. "I just happened to think of a better way."

"Great," Camino said. "Watch your head."

Thirteen

The phone directory had it listed as Jules Belmont Enterprises. It was located out of the high-rent district in nearby El Segundo, once a pleasant little beach town. The petroleum industry had now taken it over, planted derricks everywhere, belching eye-watering sulfuric fumes. East of the boulevard were small manufacturing plants. Belmont had his spread there, low concrete-block buildings handy to a usable railroad spur in back. Men one-tenth as wealthy would have picked jazzier surroundings, but I had already been told Belmont hated to throw good money away.

The old biddy inside the reception office said Belmont wasn't in. When I asked where he might be, she thought about it, as if considering giving out that information was not in her contract. Reluctantly she ventured it. "In the warehouse, I guess."

Outside, a man in overalls and white boots, untroubled by conscience, pointed to the warehouse. It was metal, with rounded sides, and could have been a hangar or Quonset hut bought as war-surplus stock at a saving. It was half crammed with wood crates. A little man was hammering on one, wheezing and cussing. He was middle-aged, wearing dirty sneakers.

I watched him beat on a few nails, then stepped up and asked him where I might find Belmont. He put down his hammer and faced me. "I'm Belmont," he croaked. "Whaddaya want?"

He wore a beat-up hat, a tattered sweater, rumpled work pants, a shirt with a frayed collar. He didn't look as if he was about to make any list of the ten best-dressed men in the country. I've seen better-dressed bums. Despite the sweater, he looked cold. He was blue-skinned, probably cyanosed; his eyes were heavy-lidded, cold and gray. His nose might have fit a bigger man. He looked about fifty going on a hundred.

I handed him my card. He waved it off. "What does it say? Can't see a damn thing without my glasses."

I began to tell him my name and mission in life. The building started to shake, accompanied by a tremendous roaring overhead. I knew I wasn't that forceful, and when Belmont tapped his ear and pointed overhead, I remembered we were near L.A. International Airport in the flight pattern of the big jumbo jets. Considering the volume of traffic and his proximity, Belmont should have been stone-deaf by this time. But again he was playing the buck. Rent had to be cheaper here. Factors of comfort and convenience didn't enter into it.

The sound waves trailed away and I tried again. "Max Roper. Private investigator."

Belmont's narrow jaw dropped. His cold eyes crinkled as he smiled. Surprising me further, he stuck out his hand for my shake. "No kidding? A private eye? You know, I've always wanted to meet one of you fellows personally."

A gambler's hand is usually soft and he sports a big star sapphire you have to be blind to miss. Belmont's hand was hard and firm; the only decoration, calluses. I asked if he had a boat at Marina del Rey called the *Dakar Doll*.

"What about it? They late with the rent?"

My first question and I was already behind. "Who's they?"

"Charter deal. Fellers I rent the boat to. They're supposed to take care of the docking charges."

"How long has your boat been chartered?"

He shrugged, grinning. "Maybe a year, off and on. Sometimes for a few days, sometimes longer. Depends on who wants that big a ship and why. Boats are an expensive investment, or maybe you didn't know that. That one cost me over a million."

I should have thought of that new growing business—rent-a-yacht services. You could tour the harbor or cruise the world in somebody else's boat. Even for millionaires, boats were a luxury, and many of them were available to rent. The crew and hors d'oeuvre came with it. All you needed was the fee and your own liquor.

"How long has the present tenant had it?"

"Can't say offhand. Couple of weeks."

"How long will he have the use of it?"

Belmont shook his head slowly. "Got me there, mister. I'd have to check my books. Could be run out right now."

"I'd appreciate that information. Can you tell me who chartered it from you?"

"Not offhand," Belmont said, looking regretful. "Got one hell of a terrible memory. Got to write everything down. I reckon it's all there with the rest of my papers."

"Maybe you'll remember this. Was there a Chinese gentleman involved with the leasing arrangement?"

"You mean the man who made the deal?"

"Either the front man or whoever took it over."

The man who toted an empire of twenty-odd related money-making businesses in his head couldn't remember if there was a Chinese involved. "No Chinese name I recall on the lease papers. As for who's on board, it's none of my business, so I never took the trouble to find out." He tapped his side pocket. "The money was good. That's all I know."

"Who takes care of your rentals—the yacht brokers at the marina?"

His dark eyebrows lifted and his cold eyes stared mockingly. "Why should I give them the commission? It ain't nothing but signing a few papers and getting the front money. I handle it myself."

Whatever his niece preached about nonattachment, her uncle had it in reverse, with money. "I'd like to see the lease if you could spare me the time, Mr. Belmont."

A truck rumbling down the ramp outside the warehouse caught his attention. Workers—brown, black and white—were converging on it. "Sure," he said. "With you in a minute."

He shuffled to the truck, talked to the workers, making sweeping gestures at the crate he had been hammering on. He came back and showed me his thumb. "This way." As I followed, he asked over his shoulder, "What's this all about?"

I remembered Belmont had made all those millions and was

probably a lot smarter than I was. He shuffled along the concrete floor, his sneakers making a soft padding sound, looking more like some harmless old eccentric than a vengeful zillionaire big-time gambler and killer.

"A friend of mine had an accident on your boat a few nights ago," I said.

He nodded, interested. "That so? 'Course, that ain't my responsibility right now, but I'd like to hear about it." He turned sharply through an open doorway. "This way."

I followed him along the corridor. We had by-passed the reluctant receptionist. Belmont stopped and threw open a door. He walked in and I followed.

It was a small room behind the warehouse, littered with boxes and paper. There were a lot of little brown-paper bags, and I figured Belmont never threw any away and saved them for the next day's lunch he would bring.

He fished around in a cardboard carton and came up with a handful of papers. "Here we are," he said. It wasn't the kind of filing system modern business management recommended, but it seemed to work for him. He leafed through the stack of papers. "What sort of accident?"

"A couple of hoods braced him in his apartment, knocked him out and took him for a ride. He woke up tied to a chair on your boat. A Chinese gentleman across the room gave him a few orders with an ultimatum. When my friend objected, he was slugged again by the bodyguards, knocked out again and taken back to his apartment."

Belmont sounded mildly outraged. "You don't say? Any idea what the order and ultimatum was—from that Chinese fellow?"

"Somehow the man on the boat knew my friend was a friend of Jo-Jo Gonzaga. Gonzaga plays basketball for the Los Angeles Lakers," I added. "That is, he used to."

"Yes, sure, I know," Belmont said, wagging his head. "Wasn't he the fellow killed the other day?"

"Yes. And that's because he didn't follow the orders given by the Chinese gent. My friend passed it on to him but Gonzaga didn't like anybody telling him what to do."

"Too bad," Belmont said, pursing his thin lips, "but good for him, anyway."

"I don't see how you can say that, sir. You see, the order was for Gonzaga not to play in the opening game against the Knicks, the New York team. If he played, he would be killed. The same thing went for my friend. If Gonzaga didn't listen to him and played, he would be killed as well."

Belmont frowned, looking puzzled. "I don't get that part of it. Was your friend killed?"

"Not yet, but they didn't set any time limit on it," I said. "It can still happen."

Belmont shook his head vigorously. "Don't like that sort of business at all. Make a deal, I say. Screw the other guy if you can before he screws you. That's just business. I don't get this killing stuff. What's the point? There's no rhyme nor reason to it. No trick to it, either."

He had found the papers he wanted. He spread them out on his desk for me to see, smoothing down a few creases picked up in his make-do filing cabinet. "Here we are," he said. He found a metal-rimmed pair of glasses and slipped them on. His finger found the signature line unerringly. "Gomez. That's the name there, ain't it?"

I looked down at the signature and couldn't quarrel. "Louis Gomez, I make it. He the tenant?"

Belmont shrugged. "He signed for the boat. Handed me a check for the money. It was certified, good as gold."

"How much was he paying?"

Belmont cocked his head and grinned at me. "Guess you got to ask a lot of questions in your line. The boat goes for a thousand a day. He wanted it for three weeks." He checked the date and glanced at his calendar. "Sonofagun," he said softly. "I got to find me a new tenant. This lease expired as of midnight, last night."

I wasn't surprised to hear it. "Does that thousand dollars a day include crew?"

"Sure. I throw that in, just like anybody else who rents out his boat. Standard is a six-man crew. Sometimes you add another man if it's a big party."

"Okay, you throw in the crew. What about guards?"

"Guards?"

"Security for your ship. Armed guards. You supply those?"

Belmont shook his head. "What the hell for? You mean I'm supposed to lay out money to look after those jerks?"

I rubbed my forehead, but it didn't help clear things inside. "I imagine for that kind of money, whoever rents your boat can take it wherever he likes?"

Belmont squinted up at me as if I had suddenly grown a little dumber. "Of course. What the hell other reason is there for renting a boat?"

"What's the range of your ship?"

"About fifteen hundred miles. It's got staterooms for twelve, a cocktail party room that'll hold fifty. It's worth the money, all right."

"Could it make it to Mexico?"

"No problem. It can make it around the world. Need to take on fuel and stock once in a while, is all."

"It's been to Mexico, then?"

"Lots of times. Mazatlan's only a thousand miles—a six- or seven-day run." He started to stack up the papers. "If you don't need these any more, I'll put them away. Part of my system, you see. Everything where it came from, everything in its place."

He started to stuff it away when I nodded. I tried not to smile at his mockery of a filing system, noting the piles of paper and bound books crowding every shelf. There was a silver-framed picture in the corner of the lower shelf, and as Belmont put his cardboard carton back, it dislodged the picture.

I caught it as it fell. The glass needed dusting, but the long-haired blonde with guileless blue eyes behind it didn't suffer any for it. She could have been his daughter but I doubted it.

I handed it over to Belmont. "Pretty girl."

"Yeah. Not bad." He blew some dust off the glass, and set it back on the shelf without a second glance.

In a career studded with wrong guesses, there's always room for one more, and I chanced it. "Your daughter?"

Belmont grinned, crooked and cocksure. "You kidding? Believe it or not, I was once married to that little girl."

I was properly surprised.

"Yeah, she was some cute cookie," Belmont was saying. "But awfully expensive. That's why I got rid of her. It's the main reason I keep her picture around. To remind me how much she cost me so I won't make the same damn-fool mistake again."

He might have been right, but she looked worth the money. I thanked Belmont for his time. When he asked what I would do about my friend's accident, I said I would have to find the tenant Gomez first. He inclined his head in silent agreement.

I found my car and turned it around. I still wasn't sure if Belmont wasn't conning me about the boat rental. But I couldn't think of a reason for his lying about his former wife. Belmont had seemed out of it, but now everything was back together, linked in curious ways. I didn't know how expensive the former Mrs. Belmont was. It wasn't a thing to bother Gonzaga.

But it bothered me because I recognized her as Joanna Burton, the blond bombshell singer from the Gin and Gaslight Club.

Fourteen

The white hull of the *Dakar Doll* glistened in the early-morning sun. The fog had gone but I was back. Everything Jules Belmont told me might have been true. It never hurt to check.

A man wearing a heavy beard and bulky sweater stood on deck smoking a cigarette while he polished some brass. He wasn't supposed to be there, but then maybe he hadn't read the lease and didn't know it. I wasn't sure if he was the same fellow I had tapped out on the upper deck, or if he was the one who had bombed me.

I stepped on board and he noticed and stopped what he was doing. He walked toward me, frowning, his hands making short no-no wigwags. His accent made him Mexican. "Sorry. Ees private sheep."

I nodded, smiling. "Señor Gomez?"

He shook his head. *"El no es aquí. Vamos!"*

I kept smiling, pulled my coat open to show him the folded sheet of paper in the inner pocket. I took it out and offered it to him. He shook his head, and I opened it, handing it to him.

He took it reluctantly. *"Qué?"* he asked.

I pushed it closer to his face. "Go ahead. Read it. *La carta es para Señor Gomez.*"

He held it closer to his eyes, trying to make out he could read. It wasn't really a letter for Mr. Gomez, as I had told him, but instead a monthly form letter from a local Cadillac dealer who wanted me to drop in and test-drive the new model.

The logo Cad crest on top of the sheet looked impressive

enough to engage the man's attention. He shook his head sooner than I expected because he knew his reading limitations better than I. *"Hombre!"* he said apologetically, handing it back.

Smiling understandingly, I reached for it. My right arm kept going and encircled his neck instead. My left hand was on his right sleeve, pulling it down. I leaned forward, pivoted, and twisted. His body went over my back and right side, my waist serving as an axle revolving like a wheel. It's called "Loin Wheel" (Koshiguruma), and he fell heavily, still holding the dummy letter. I gave him a knife-hand strike to the face (shuto gammen-uchi), catching him on the temple. He sighed and lay still face down on the deck.

I tied his hands behind him with his belt. It had all happened faster than it takes to tell, but I checked the immediate area, anyway. Apparently casual witnesses were not about. I headed for the cabin doorway and went down the steps hoping nobody below was awake, aware, and had a gun on me.

There were six staterooms and they were all empty. Nobody was in the galley or at the wheel. I made for the big room where I'd been busted up a few times.

It wasn't occupied, and Belmont had told the truth. It definitely was a cocktail-party room that could hold fifty. What puzzled me was that was precisely what it was now. A cocktail-party room!

I looked across the room vainly for the big desk that wasn't there. The sofa and soft chairs I remembered from the bad night previous had gone, too, as had the small hard chair I had sat on twice, once on my own. The wall panels were still expensive wood but the paintings were missing.

I looked under my feet for the carpet. It had mysteriously fallen under a bad witch's spell and turned into a shining floor of wall-to-wall linoleum!

I sat down on one of the small party chairs now lining the wall. I wasn't drunk, stoned, or daydreaming. I made up for that by being hopelessly confused. I looked out the window and saw the same marina view. It was the same ship, the *Dakar Doll,* moored at the same slip. This was the only really large room on it. I slipped out the door and ran around in a circle to make certain. It was, and I came back for the last time and the last look.

A dry bar now stood where the desk had been, and two small card tables were placed next to it. They would hold the glasses and mixes for the party. I knew I'd been had but felt pretty good about it. Somebody had gone to a lot of trouble and moved very fast. If the lease wasn't up, the jig was. I couldn't prove now what I had set out to do, but I had jolted somebody into action.

I remembered the crewman I had laid out on the upper deck. He might know where I could find the lease signer Gomez. Gomez could lead me to the Chinese importer Belmont couldn't remember.

I hurried back up, running a lot of rudimentary Spanish phrases through my mind so that I wouldn't waste his time. I wanted information. *Quiero informes* would do for openers.

I had to settle for *"Por Dios!"* Somehow my karate magic had weakened. The crewman had regained his senses, unhobbled his hands, put the belt back on his pants, and gone!

Somebody was approaching along the slatted dock walk. I heard quick steps, soft and purposeful, and ducked behind the cabin housing. The footsteps echoed closer, didn't hesitate, and in another moment I had company.

It was a better day for surprises than I had expected. The new sea dog passed me by without spotting me. I made her out at five-seven, about 125. The rest was 38-27-37, and given those statistics, a girl could get by. She had given up the pants for a shortie dress today, and I had to wonder why a girl with such terrific legs would ever want to hide them. I had other things to wonder about, too. She had told me she hardly ever saw her uncle, convinced me easily, and I wondered again if I really knew anything.

I waited until she had gone below and then I carefully followed, to find out what she was up to. I gave her a little time. The engines didn't start up and that eliminated her stealing the boat. I peeked through the port window and made her out in the cocktail-party room. She was being very thorough and business-like, moving along from chair to chair, lifting the chair pads, dropping them and moving on. She came to the card tables, lifted the cloth covering, let it go and went to the dry bar. She got behind it but didn't fix herself a drink.

She stepped out shaking her head and looking puzzled, and I felt happy to see somebody else in the same bind. I ducked away as she came out. She went through the staterooms in good time. I heard things moving and dropping at a good steady pace. She went from there to the galley. I heard pots and pans but didn't detect any smell of cooking. That eliminated her catering the party room.

I was up on deck when she came out. She had something under her arm, and I was the only remaining puzzled person on the ship. It was a brown-paper bag, but I had that nice clear feeling, known only to the better operators, of certainty. I knew her uncle hadn't asked her to come down there to pick up his lunch.

She stopped when she saw me, and it didn't take too long for her to recognize me and smile. "Mr. Roper, don't tell me you're here again! I thought you were going to send Uncle his bill."

"I got to thinking the mail would take too long."

"You wasted your time," she said. "Nobody's here."

"*You* are," I said pointedly. "I thought you told me you kept away from your uncle and that evil aura of money. What happened to that I AM-ness system?"

"The element of Self," she said, "is Being, not having. I'm only running an errand."

I pointed to the paper bag she held. "What's in it?"

She glanced down at it. "Nothing very important."

"It wouldn't be some bags of fine white powder?"

"Powder?"

"It's worth a lot of money. It's called heroin."

She registered astonishment and did it very well. "What are you talking about?"

"It retails for almost a quarter of a million a kilo. It comes up from Mexico sometimes."

Her eyes were saucers, only prettier. "Mexico?"

"On its way over from Marseilles or Istanbul or Thailand."

86

She stared. "Are you feeling all right? I'd almost forgotten that nasty crack you had on your head last night."

"It's better now. All healed up. If it wasn't, I wouldn't be half as suspicious."

"I'm really glad you're better," she said. "You had me worried."

"It's different now. It's your turn to have me worried. What's in the bag?"

She backed up a step, then smiled. "Oh, I get it. You're back to your professional self today—the private detective."

"I think that's my real I AM-ness. I can't seem to get the hang of un-becoming one."

"There are a few principles you have to remember, Mr. Roper. I mentioned one last night. Renouncing the object of the ego's craving. Another one is letting go of all possessiveness."

"Are there any more I have to remember?"

"Recognizing the Being of others."

"Sounds good. Any more?"

"Owning things without being owned by them." She glanced at her watch. "You'll have to work at it. It's not easy."

"It will be a lot easier for me after I find out what's in that paper bag you're holding."

"You're just unconsciously resisting," she said. "Not trying to change. I'm trying to help you find your real Self. The inner you. The Self that's always there watching you, never changing."

"That one is working fine," I said. "Right now it's watching me very closely to make sure I don't let you get away with that paper bag." She tapped one foot of a beautiful leg, showing vast discontent and a lot of what I was missing. "Okay, I'll make it easier for you, Miss Belmont. What are you doing here on your uncle's boat?"

"Oh," she said nervously. "I see what you mean. You mean, like what am I doing here?"

I nodded. "Like."

Her hair didn't need sweeping back but she had a go at it just the same. She had nice rounded arms, I noticed.

"Would that question be in the nature of your business?"

"I give you my word on it."

"Okay," she said, coming to an instant decision. "My uncle called me."

"But he doesn't, usually."

"That's true. That's what was so surprising about the whole thing. I haven't spoken to him in—well, like years."

"Okay. He missed you. What did he want?"

"Want? He asked me if I could do him a small favor."

I nodded to give her assurance. "Like what kind of a favor?"

"He asked me to come down here and see if I could find some party masks."

"Party masks?" I echoed. "Is he giving a party?"

"I don't know. I suppose. I didn't think of asking. But that's why I'm here. I figured it wouldn't take much time, and I'm practically in the neighborhood—"

"But you didn't find any party masks," I said.

Her eyes widened. "But I did! They're kind of queer-looking, but I guess they're party masks. I mean, what else could they be?"

She reached inside the bag and showed me what she had in her hand. She was right, in a way. They were kind of queer-looking. If I had to guess, I'd have to put them down as party masks, too.

One was a gorilla. The second was a rube. The third was a wolfman.

"Well? What's so funny?" she demanded.

Fifteen

Camino shoved a stick of gum in his mouth. "I hope these are on the level," he said. "I'd hate to think of you going to all that trouble rounding up three masks just to prove your point."

"The only trouble I had was in convincing Belmont's niece we needed them for evidence."

Camino lifted his eyebrows. "We?"

"They came off the same boat, Nick. Owned by Belmont. The *Dakar Doll.* Same one the hoods brought me to, and where I got the order from the Chinese gent from Burma."

"So you say," Camino said. "But if Belmont leased his boat to outsiders, he's not responsible. Which brings me to my point. Evidence of what? Nobody else heard your story, which makes it hearsay, not admissible in court. You say they picked you up, knocked you out, gave you an ultimatum. A man in your line gets a lot of that treatment. I can't see the D.A. getting excited over it."

"But those are the guys who knocked off Gonzaga."

"Prove it," Camino said. "I'd like to believe it. All you have to do is find them and bring them in."

"That all?"

"Alive would be better."

It took me two lights to realize I was being tailed. I let them come up and didn't try to lose them. They weren't novices and held back, merely keeping in touch. I tried to make out the guy at the wheel; it could have been the crewman I busted. The man beside him wore a hat, not too popular an item with the Angeleno natives.

I swung away from downtown traffic and cut right, letting out a little. They jumped the car between us and came on fast, trying to close the gap. I led them toward Little Tokyo and worried them some jumping a light. They were close behind me as I swung off Los Angeles Street into an alley. I knew the alley was dead-end, if they didn't. I braked fast and swung the heap around and when they came in I had them before they knew it.

They had come in swinging wide on the right side and I drove my heap right at them, pinning them to the alley wall. I had my hand out, my gun on the driver's nose. The man on his right couldn't do a thing about it.

"Drop it!" I said, and he dropped it. The driver was the crewman I had surprised earlier. His eyes were frightened, but not very many are happy looking into a gun. "Where's Gomez?" I asked.

His eyes rolled, trying to find the man on his right. I leaned in the open window and pulled him closer to the muzzle. The extra inch didn't make him any deader than he was before, but when you're bullying somebody the little tricks help. "Gomez," I repeated. "You speak English?"

He managed a sickly smile. "*Sí, señor*. I spik."

I felt a little stupid waving the gun, but then I remembered Gonzaga. He hadn't even had that favor. "I'm looking for Señor Gomez. Louis Gomez. He rented that ship."

The other man leaned forward nervously. "Please, señor. Don't shoot. I am Gomez."

I swung the gun to cover him better. "First, why are you tailing me? What do you want?"

His eyes pleaded. "Please, señor. It was nothing personal. We have orders, you understand."

"Fine," I said. "Who gave the orders?" They looked at one another, obviously more frightened than ever. I made a big show of looking at my wristwatch. "Ten seconds. What's the name of the Chinese man—and where can I find him?"

They exchanged glances again and whispered in Spanish

too fast for me. The driver wiped his mouth. "Eef we tell you, he keel us."

"Maybe not," I said. "Maybe I keel heem first."

They thought about it and shrugged in tandem. Lopez was first. "His name is Mr. Wu. A very bad man."

"I know. He killed a friend of mine."

"We don't know about that, señor. We just have to do with ship." He waved his hands. "Make lease. Bring money."

"What else did you bring—a load of heroin?"

He looked at me sadly. "Please, señor. I know nothing. *Por favor!*"

It wasn't my scene, anyway. "Okay. Stop stalling. Where's Wu?"

The crewman cleared his throat. "*No es aquí, señor.* He go back. *May-hee-co.*"

"*Diga! Diga!*" I said. "*En todo.* Where? *En donde?*"

Lopez leaned forward. His throat had to be dry from fear. But I could understand his whispering. "He is in Nuevo Laredo, señor."

"*Es algo. Qué casa?*" I asked.

He pointed to his coat. I nodded and he opened it. An envelope protruded from an inner pocket. I let him hand it to me. It was an airmail special from Nuevo Laredo. The return address told me where I could find the mysterious Mr. Wu.

Maybe with luck the other three would be there.

The gorilla, the rube and the wolfman.

It's a typical border town. The main drag, Guerrerro Avenue, is like something out of early Republic Studios or MGM. Bazaars teeming with the tourists looking for tax-free booze, cut-rate jewelry, handcrafted junk.

They miss out on the true specialties. Narcotic traffic and corpses. That's what Nuevo Laredo really deals in—drugs and death. They favor the machine gun and machete.

It's the heart of the smuggling chain, the principal Mexican connection. The Texas-Mexican border along the Rio Grande offers 1,200 miles for the smuggling of heroin, opium, cocaine and marijuana into the United States. The major narcotics thoroughfare goes north from Mexico City and Monterrey via Highway 85, straight for the valley of Texas.

The international bridge into Laredo, Texas, carries a swarm of thousands of pedestrians and cars a day from the Mexican state of Tamaulipas. Some Mexican federal agents look the other way, and it's a sieve for smugglers. If they don't dare the bridge, they can always ford the Rio with backpack and a good hustling spirit.

The Belmont kid called me before I left. She reported she had followed my instructions and told her uncle there were no party masks to be found on his boat.

"I told a big lie for you," she said. "Generally I'm a very truthful person."

"Maybe it's because you're young," I said. "It gets easier as you go along."

"It must be your line of work that makes you so cynical," she said. "Have you given any more thought to your I AM-ness?"

"I'd like to, but I'm very busy. I have to go out of town."

"Where?"

"Mexico."

"Mexico? Why on earth are you going there?"

"I think I have to kill a couple of fellows."

"What if they kill you first?"

"They're not supposed to. I'm the hero type. Like Bogart, remember?"

"Well, if you're still alive, hurry back. I want to sell you something."

"Don't tell me he has you pushing the stuff now."

"I'm talking about a painting. One of mine."

"Why would you want to sell me a painting?"

"I need the money."

The small charter plane found a spot it liked on the airstrip. We taxied to the end, where I found a car-rental outfit. I surrendered a lot of money and they let me have a beat-up Mustang and a handful of maps. I had already told the pilot when to expect me for the return trip, allowing myself enough of a spread and not drawing it too fine.

"Watch yourself if you hit any of the local bars," he told me. "They got a lot of the ranch-hand *pistoleros* in there, and they all have guns under their belts."

"Who's got most of the action?" I asked.

He looked at me. "There used to be two rival gangs—the Reyes Prunedas and the Gayton Clan. It's been pretty hot and heavy between their ranches. But I understand a few independents have moved in."

I said that happened to be my understanding, too.

"Watch yourself," he said. "I hate to fly all the way back solo."

There had to be a lot of local feuding for the biggest piece of the lucrative border drug stream. I didn't know Wu's connections, but it was a lot better than even money he had to have a lot of *pistoleros*.

I looked at the envelope Gomez had handed me. The return address wasn't a casa but a ranch. Rancho Rosales.

Driving slowly through the main drag, I counted the bars and saloons. They added up to a lot of drunken heads. I felt thirsty, found one that looked clean, and parked.

I changed my mind suddenly and remained behind the wheel. Three men were swaggering out of the bar. They were big guys and they weren't wearing masks, but I thought I knew them.

The dude in the middle was swarthy and pockmarked. A livid scar was a memento traveling the left side of his jaw. He was thick-shouldered and broad in the chest. His arms didn't hang particularly low but I figured him for the gorilla.

The man on his left was light-haired, straw-colored.

The rube. Lloyd.

The other man was bigger than either of them, six-two or more, and I couldn't see if one of his hands was missing its middle finger. But two out of three made it easier. He had to be the wolfman, the third man I'd never seen. The baby who always managed to zonk my head in from behind.

I could have gunned them all down from where I was sitting and been off and away. It would have been a satisfactory feeling. But I wanted more out of my trip and my day.

I wanted Wu.

The three men piled into a station wagon and took off. I let them have a little headway before pulling out, driving slowly through the town, marking them well ahead. Past the hovels and squatter huts spread out in squalor, where people still lived like animals, the road narrowed. Traffic going south was light and I let them build their lead up to a mile.

They cut left and east at a junction. A road gang up ahead near a little bridge was halting cars, allowing north and south traffic through alternately on the one-lane bridge. I slowed and let the station wagon go on ahead. The Mex in charge of waving cars through tried to hurry me. I stalled, and he came running up holding his slow-down flag marked *lento*. I looked sheepish, ran the engine with the ignition key off, only the starter working. He listened patiently for a moment, then turned, exasperated, and waved his flag at the other man across the bridge.

A rickety old yellow bus came through from the other side, a van and a donkey cart. The station wagon was now far enough ahead for me to risk it, and I had the car ready and idling when it came my turn again. "*Ándale! Ándale!*" he yelled, and when I passed him, he spat out the word "*Gringo!*"

The valley was capped by red hills rolling gently on either side of the road. In the distance they towered gray and formidable. A few spavined horses watched me go by without much interest. The pasture was marked off with barbed wire, the ranch house set well behind the highway. The wagon ahead of me turned south abruptly and it was easy to follow them by the funnel of billowing sand and dust they left behind.

Five and one-tenth miles from the bridge they turned west, briefly south and west again. I followed the yellow cloud of sand and dust. I made the last turn, and they were gone.

I maintained the same pace. There were Keep Off signs

posted: *No Entrar!* On my right dust was slow in settling. The opening was a huge gateway with an overhanging beam arch marked RANCHO ROSALES. A white-clad man wearing a sombrero was closing the gate. He carried a rifle and packed a double band of ammo around his waist and across one shoulder. As I continued past I made out the station wagon parked in a wide circular gravel driveway. Next to it were two gleaming black sedans, late-model Cads. The three men were walking across the drive toward the main ranch house.

It was white, two stories high, with balconies set Spanish-style front and back. Behind were low outlying buildings. Bunkhouses, barn, workshop, storerooms. The hired guns, the tough *pistoleros*, drifters from the interior farmlands looking for a quick and steady buck would be here. Wu would be in the main wing with his own strong-arm men, the three I was after. If Rosales was still alive and around, he would have taken on a new partner. If he was smart, his personal guard would also be handy.

A high wall surrounded the grounds. Farther along, the fencing became strands of wire. I could make out riders in the distance posted at the outer perimeters. It was a big spread separated from the distant hills by a dry creek bed half hidden by a grove of willows.

The ranch house had a commanding view of the immediate terrain. Its flaw was the creek behind the trees where a man could find cover.

Some solid streaks of gold in the sky were still resisting the oncoming of dusk. The solitary riders would be leaving their posts soon to return to the ranch area for chow. I found a jutting clay cliff wall around a turn and parked the Mustang off the road under its overhang.

Twilight came on quickly. When its purple mantle permitted, I was in the creek bed trying not to twist my ankle on the hundreds of loose rocks scattered along its length. It was going to be a clear, cold night. I moved along carefully.

All I needed was a plan to do what I had to and come out of it alive. It couldn't be foolproof because there were too many intangibles. My mind went back to Gonzaga being caught dead to rights that early morning on his own balcony, and I wondered if the killer had had to make do, too, or if his plan had already been set and foolproof.

Somebody like Wu wouldn't have needed to plot it closely. All he had to do was put the plan into operation and leave it to the judgment of the killer with the long-range rifle.

I pictured the three hoods in the house now, remembering how they had swaggered out of the town saloon. Somehow they seemed strictly to type, the kind of muscle every kingpin carries around with him, good at the strong-arming, close-quarter work. For the first time I felt a disquieting qualm. The rifle was a different line of work, calling for another type of killer. One who liked to work alone and at long-range.

He would be cool, disdainful of masks, proud of his skill, a deadly marksman at any distance. But that was his key. He liked to work at a distance. I already knew, too late, this man wouldn't be in the ranch house living it up with the rest of the hired help. He had to be a loner.

The bunkhouse had quieted down. Moments later the lights went out. I was out of the creek, sticking to the shadow of the main house. The guard at the gate slumped in his chair, his rifle across his lap. He could have been sleeping but I wasn't sure. The lights were still on in the ranch house. I heard voices, none of them in singsong pidgin English.

Two large trucks were parked side by side opposite the bunkhouse. They might have come in while I was waiting in the creek behind the house. They might have been hidden in the barn and were coming out now for a midnight run. Heavy wooden crates were stacked near the tailgates. They weren't ready for loading yet, apparently, and the drivers were doing sacktime, I imagined, preparatory for their run. They could have been carrying farm machinery, soft drinks or hard drugs. My inclination was toward the latter. You didn't need a gang of *pistoleros* to muscle in the other items.

I stuck my gun in the gate guard's ear. "*Buenas noches! Dónde está el señor Rosales?*"

His eyes flicked sadly down to the rifle on his lap. He raised his hands slowly. "*Muerto!*" he said softly. He drew a dusky hand slowly across his throat to show me how dead Rosales really was.

"*Gracias. Qué vergüenza!*"

His eyes rolled. Admitting it was a shame, he bobbed his head slightly. "*Sí, señor. Un hombre grande.*"

"*Sí. Pobre de él!*" I wasn't sure it was that great a pity.

"*Sí.*"

I showed him the gun. "*El señor Wu es por aquí?*"

"*Sí, señor. En la casa.*"

"*Con los tres hombres?*"

"*Sí, señor.*"

"*Quiénes están allí?*" I was wondering who else was around.

He shook his head as much as the gun permitted. "*Es todo, señor.* Nobody else. *Los tres hombres. El gordo chino.*"

I didn't know Wu was fat. "*El señor Wu es el primer señor aquí?*"

He said, "*Sí, señor,*" admitting Wu was number one there.

I asked him about the hired guns, the *pistoleros*. He spat and told me they were drunk or sleeping, or both. I pointed to the trucks and asked where the drivers were. Asleep, he said. I asked if they were due to pull out later.

"*Sí,*" he said. "*Medianoche.*"

There was still a little while to go before midnight. I looked at the gun in my hand, and the guard could read me. He took his sombrero off to make it easier. I shook my head. He shivered. "*Por favor, señor!*"

I didn't see any point to clobbering him over the head. After I was gone, whoever was left would wake him up and then kill him. I took out my billfold instead and gave him one of the larger ones. "*Ándale! Vamos!* Scram!"

He pocketed it and replaced his sombrero on his head. "*Gracias, señor.* Now that you have decided against killing me, perhaps I can help you. Permit me to introduce myself."

I was better prepared to blow the bill than hear the almost impeccable English. "Go ahead," I said. "Maybe it's worth it."

"My name is Manuel Melendez. I am a Mexican federal agent. Mr. Wu does not know, of course, that I have been placed here to investigate the murder of Antonio Rosales."

"It figures. What else do you want to tell me?"

"You speak rotten Spanish."

"Okay, so now we both know it. I've got some urgent business in there myself with Wu and his three playmates."

"You are with the Bureau?"

"Private investigator from L.A. A friend was killed there a few nights ago. I think it was Wu and his hoods."

Melendez nodded. "It is possible. Wu and the other men were away for a week. They returned only last night."

"Good. That proves a point. Do I crab your act by going in there?"

"Not if you don't kill Mr. Wu. The Mexican government is interested in his activities. I am personally responsible to the head of the Mexican Federal Police Commandant, Colonel Perales." He picked up his rifle. "I cannot expose my position, you understand. But perhaps I can cover you in some way."

I took something out of my pocket. "This might be all the cover I need."

Melendez brought his torch closer and stared.

I knocked politely at the front door of the ranch house. Somebody walked across the room in high-heeled boots. The door was thrown open and I stepped inside.

"Trick or treat," I said.

The man who opened the door took a step back, his light-blue eyes stared. He probably wasn't expecting a man wearing the awesome green mask of Frankenstein's monster.

"Lloyd?" I asked pleasantly, and kicked the door shut behind my back. "No rube mask tonight?"

The other two were out of their chairs fast. The one at the far end on my left was the big burly man. Directly ahead in front of the fireplace was the wider stockier one, swarthy and pockmarked, the scar welt running up his jawline.

I nodded pleasantly to him. "You were the gorilla, right?" He stiffened, hunching his shoulders, and I showed him the gun in my hand. He froze, and I put it on the big man to my left.

"Raise your hands. I want to count your fingers." He glowered but they went up slowly, fingers flexing. "Sonofagun!

There's one finger missing on your left hand! That makes you the wolfman, correct?"

His eyes darted to a rifle over the fireplace. I waved my gun to dissuade him. He stopped where he was but Lloyd was faster than I expected. He lunged in with a sudden move and knocked the gun out of my hand. It bounced off the door behind me and as he dived for it I chopped at the side of his head with my open hand. I caught him a little too high but hard enough to send him spinning off to my right. He fell over a table and by the time he got up I had kicked the gun between my feet.

It took only a split second to secure the gun there, but when I looked up they had all moved closer. They were good at this game.

It was a classic situation now. The wolfman directly on my left. The rube on my right. Ahead of me the barrel-chested, heavy-shouldered man who had worn the gorilla mask.

"Where's Wu?" I asked, not really expecting an answer.

"He'll be right down," Lloyd said softly, "to pick up the pieces, Roper. You're as good as dead right now, pal, only you don't know it."

He made his move quickly. I gave him side thrust kick with right leg (yoko geri kekomi) smashing hard into his spleen.

It must have hurt, because he screamed.

The wolfman snarled on my left. Moving fast for a big man, he came in hooking his right low. I used left forefist middle outside block (seiken chudan soto-uke) and moving counter clockwise followed with a roundhouse kick from my right leg to his neck-jaw area (mae washi geri). His neck snapped with an ugly sound. Eyes spinning, he went to his knees, gasping.

The gorilla with the pockmarked face roared in, throwing an overhand right. I continued smoothly spinning counterclockwise in the movements once charted for me by my karateka friend and *sensei* back East, Malachi Lee. I wasn't as graceful or fluid but my back kick with left leg (ushiro geri) was accurate and caught my man hard in the solar plexus region. He grunted, discovered suddenly he had a smashed rib cage and severe internal damage, and pitched to the floor.

That made three down and one to go when an inner door was opened suddenly. A little fat man with black hair and a ragged mustache stepped into the room and took in the scene without expression. He quickly backed out, slamming the door shut. "Wu!" I yelled and went across the room for him. I heard a lock snap and the lights went out. I stumbled over the wolfman, and he didn't object. When I got to the door it was locked tight. It was solid, at least two inches thick, a good Spanish door, and all I could do with it was bruise my shoulder. I clawed the wall and couldn't find the wall light switch. Outside a car engine turned over. Tires screeched and spit gravel. It roared past, heading for the gate.

The fed agent Melendez was there and I hoped would blow his cover and stop Wu. I didn't hear anything but the sound of the revved-up car roaring away.

I stepped over limp bodies and found the front door. The gate was open. As I ran down the front steps, I could see twin red taillights receding in the distance. In another moment they were gone.

Melendez, the undercover federal agent, sat slumped on his chair, the way I had found him. I couldn't figure the man going to sleep again and I grabbed his shoulder and shook him roughly. He fell forward without a sound. My hand felt warm and sticky and then I saw the long-bladed knife deep in his throat.

Somehow the *pistoleros* in the bunkhouse were still asleep. I went back to the house and found a wall switch. They were still on the floor where I had left them. The wolfman was dead, his head twisted grotesquely to one side. I stooped over the gorilla man, and he was finished with breathing, too, as dead as the other. I stepped quickly over to Lloyd.

He lay on his side, gasping, hands braced on the floor, trying to get off. He looked more like a dying man now than the playful fun-loving rube. I jerked his head up by his short hair and leaned close. "This is Roper, Lloyd. Who killed Gonzaga?"

His eyes stared back at me, lusterless, without comprehension. A spasm of pain made him writhe. His blue eyes narrowed into focus. He tried to raise one hand off the floor to give me the thumb. "Up yours, Jack!" he croaked. His eyes rolled back into his head, and then he was dead, too.

100

Sixteen

"Not bad," Camino said. "You killed off everybody who didn't matter and flushed the head man of the operation."

"Don't worry," I said. "I'll find Wu."

"If you do, it will be one hell of an encore. Maybe you ought to try using your gun instead of all that karate. We need somebody alive and able to talk. You're still of the opinion Wu killed Gonzaga?"

"If he didn't pull the trigger, he gave the order," I said. "Maybe he's got another hired gun, a man good with a rifle. It all started with Wu. Who else could have done it?"

"I didn't," Camino said wearily. "And I know you didn't. That only leaves the rest of the world. Gonzaga had a lot of friends. Maybe he also had a few enemies."

"Belmont is still a possible. He was married to Joanna Burton for a while. Still keeps her picture around. Maybe he shared a common syndrome. Didn't like the idea of his wife going for a Mex like Gonzaga."

Camino stubbed out his butt and blew smoke through his nose. "I like that one too. I like them all. Also, I like a little proof."

"Why don't you like Belmont for it—because he's so rich?"

"It's a factor," Camino admitted. "With his kind of dough, he could afford dames like Burton every day of the year and never miss it."

"He said he got rid of her because she was too expensive. Could be he was still hung up on her."

"Not a guy like Belmont," Camino said. "His only hang-up is money. How the hell do you think he got it all? But, as you know, I happen to be very broad-minded in my thinking. If you want me to think it was Belmont—"

"I know," I cut in. "Prove it."

Camino nodded and took his feet off his desk. "Nice seeing you. What was the name of that Mexican Police Commandant the agent Melendez was working for?"

"Colonel Perales."

Camino sighed and drew his phone closer. "He's been calling. You signed for a car in Nuevo Laredo. I've got to do a little fast talking to convince him you didn't cut his man's throat."

I got up, feeling very tired. "How do you know I didn't?"

Camino shrugged. "All that karate jazz. You laid them all out with your feet. You need good hands to throw a knife. Also, if you'd used your head instead of thinking through your feet, maybe you wouldn't have to start all over again now."

It was Friday morning. It seemed as good a time as any to hit the sack and make up some lost sleep. I was doing pretty well when the phone rang. It was Buzz Bryant, the Laker coach.

"Thought you'd be interested," he said. "Ellis Decker is missing."

"You said missing?"

"Right. Maybe he'll show up in time. The third game of the series starts tonight. We got shoved back a little so the TV people could fit us in with prime time."

"When did you see Decker last?"

"Last practice session late yesterday. He went back to the hotel with the other guys. He went out later, saying he had something to do, wouldn't take long."

"Never showed up for bed check?"

"No."

I remembered young Decker's feelings about women, the idea he could be as big a stud as Gonzaga. "He could be shacking up with a broad."

"I know," Bryant said. "But he didn't show up for this

morning's practice run-through. That's why I thought you'd be interested."

"What time is it there now?"

"We're running three hours later than you. It's a little after noon. Game time is eight-thirty—New York time."

"What hotel are you at?"

"The Chase. West Side at 38th. Near the Garden."

"Have you called the police?"

"Not yet."

"I'll catch the next plane out."

I hung up, showered and got dressed. I checked the airlines, found an open spot leaving soon, and started throwing some things into a bag. The phone rang again.

It was the I AM-ness twiggie. Belmont's niece.

"When did you get back?" she asked forthrightly.

"A little while ago."

"How was Mexico? Did you kill anybody?"

"Only three. The fourth got away."

She laughed. "I've got to talk to you sometime when you're serious. And I've picked out a very nice painting for you. When would you like to come over and see it?"

"It can't be now. I'm leaving for New York."

"You can't be," she wailed. "You only just got back."

"I know, but you know us private eyes. Always on the go."

"When are you leaving?"

"Just as soon as you hang up."

"Honestly? Wait, I think I have an idea." The phone was silent for a moment. Then she came on again. "Listen, I've got nothing else to do. How about if I picked you up and drove you to the airport?"

I glanced at my watch. There was still a little time. "You don't have to. Why trouble yourself?"

"It's no trouble," she said. "I like talking to you."

"Okay," I said. "Can you make it inside a half-hour?"

"I'm close by. I can be there in ten."

"All right." I started to read off my address, but she interrupted, telling me she had it. "How do you know where I live?"

She laughed again. "I copied it down from your billfold. Remember, when you were unconscious for so long?"

"I think it's becoming a natural condition," I said. "Meet you downstairs."

I told my answering service where I'd be, finished packing, and was down in front of my building when she came roaring up. She was driving a little pink VW with the slide-top canvas roof open. She swooped into the curb like a kamikaze pilot without mounting the curb or taking my legs off.

I threw my bag over on the rear seat and got in. She had it in gear and in the middle of the street in less than two seconds. Screaming brakes sounded behind. "It's always a good idea to look before you pull out from a curb," I said.

"I suppose," she said, "but you'd be surprised at how many people have good brakes in this town."

She took the next turn without compassion and I saw it was going to be that kind of ride and settled back. She was wearing something yellow and very short and it was more fun watching her than her driving. She headed for the freeway and I closed my eyes momentarily when she hit the on-ramp. The driver of the big diesel truck had seen it all before. He hit his air brakes and let her go by. I looked back; and he was shaking his head, grinning.

A mile up ahead a driver changed lanes. "Just look at that rotten driver," the girl said. "He didn't even signal."

"It's probably not his day," I said. "Some signal on even days, some on the odd ones." She grimaced and looked better at it than most girls smiling.

"Whatever happened to those party masks I gave you?"

"The party's over," I said. "Those are the three jokers I killed."

She glanced at me quickly. "Something tells me you're not joking. Is that what really happened down there?"

"It's what happened. I didn't set out to kill them deliberately. That's the way it worked out."

The gaiety went out of her voice. "Was this all because of your friend—the one you said was killed?"

"Yes, one thing led to another. They were hoods and would

104

have been knocked off eventually, anyway, by some other tough operator. They just got what they've been dealing out themselves most of their lives."

She chewed on her lower lip. "I don't understand," she said. "What's all this got to do with my uncle? You got zonked on his boat and thrown off unconscious, to drown. You were back on it again yesterday when I found the masks. What were you looking for?"

"I wasn't sure, but anyway, you found part of it."

"Those masks? But what's that to do with my uncle?"

"I'm not sure, yet. He told me he rented his boat out on a charter to some other fellows. One of that group was the one who killed my friend Gonzaga."

"The basketball player? But why?" She took her hands off the wheel to clasp them against her chest. "He was beautiful!"

The VW didn't go along much worse without her hands guiding it. "A lot of women thought so," I said. "Just how well do you know your uncle?"

She got her hands back at the helm, swerving it out of the lane it had found. "I told you. Not well at all. We just never found anything compatible to talk about, I guess."

"Did you ever get to know his wife?"

"Which one?"

"How many did he have?"

"Three, I think. Or maybe it was four. Like that. Why?"

"The only one I know about is Joanna Burton. She sings down at the Gin and Gaslight Club."

She clapped her hands together. "Oh, sure, I remember her. They weren't married very long, you know. It broke up kind of sudden."

"How long did it last?"

"Only a few months. Why?"

"How long ago, do you remember?"

"Well, she was the last. About two years ago, I guess. Why?"

"You asked how your uncle might be connected. She was Jo-Jo Gonzaga's girl at the time he was killed."

She looked at me, curious. "So what does that prove?"

"I don't know. Maybe your uncle was jealous."

She laughed merrily. "I can see you don't really know Uncle Jules. I don't think he has an emotion in his bones."

"I didn't know they came in bones," I said. "Gonzaga was a Mexican, you know. The possibility entered my mind that your rich uncle, like a few other liberal-minded folk, just couldn't cotton to the idea of his ex shacking up with a Chicano."

"Maybe," she said. "But you're forgetting something else that could be just as important."

"Lay it on me."

"If you've seen Joanna, you should know. A lot of men flip over her. Gonzaga wasn't the only one."

"Okay," I said. "It figures. But I was referring specifically to the fact he was a Mexican. Maybe her being with other men didn't bother him as much."

"I already told you," she said patiently, "nothing really ever bothered Uncle Jules. As for the rest of your theory, could you see yourself going for Joanna?"

I shrugged. "It's possible."

She slammed on her brakes, and my head didn't go through the windshield. "Get out!" she said firmly.

I looked at her dumbly. "What's wrong?"

"Nothing," she said. "We're here! You're leaving on American Airlines, aren't you?"

The airline was there just outside my window. I'd been so occupied watching her up-shift and down-shift and cut off cars, I'd lost sight of the route. I grunted assent, lifted my bag off the rear seat, opened my door and stepped to the curb. She stepped out of her side and walked around the front of her VW to join me. It looked like another chance to say goodbye and I put my bag down and turned.

The gunshot sounded as I moved, and I ducked, pulling the girl down by her arm. The bullet whined and ricocheted off the car hood with a loud metallic sound. It spent itself harmlessly against the concrete side of the terminal building.

Across the street was a big parking lot. A car revved up, tore off behind other cars and disappeared. There were exits at the far end, and chasing after it was futile.

"It's okay," I said, helping her up.

She was probably frightened but she looked angry. "Was that somebody shooting?" I nodded. "At us?" I bowed. She glared. "You probably are a dangerous person, at that. Somebody was trying to kill you!"

"It's a fun game," I said, the same dry taste in my mouth.

Her eyes followed mine to the deep furrow where the bullet had plowed its way across her hood. It marked a line that was exactly between the girl and me.

She found her voice at last. "Somebody must have been following us." She looked around. "Or waiting for you here."

"That's what puzzles me," I said. "Apart from you, the Laker coach in New York City and the airlines ticket computer, nobody knew I was making this plane."

"That sounds like a puzzler, all right."

"It was a sudden decision I made hardly a minute before you phoned." A bolt of lightning made its way reluctantly into my brain. "Where were you when you called?"

She shrugged carelessly. "What difference would that make?"

"I don't know yet. Where were you?"

She took a deep breath and exhaled slowly. It was a lovely sight but I was more interested in her answer. "I called from my uncle's office."

"Uncle Jules in El Segundo? The one you hardly ever see?" She nodded shyly each time. "How come? I thought you two didn't have anything in common."

"Well," she said. "I did have to tell him a whopper about those masks you wouldn't let me bring over to him. Maybe he didn't believe my story. Anyway, he called and said he wanted to see me over there right away."

"What was so urgent? What did he want?"

Her dark-blue eyes didn't waver from mine. "He asked if I knew you. And if I did know you, how did it happen, and where and how long ago."

"What did you tell him?"

"The truth."

I picked up my bag. "That's that, then. Thanks for the lift. I'll be seeing you."

"I told him," she said, "that it was absolutely none of his business."

"And it was after that you phoned me?"

"Yes."

I put the bag down.

"What are you doing?" she asked.

"Trying to dig this .22 bullet out of the wall."

"I saved your life and gave you my best brandy and drove you all the way down here," she said. "Aren't you going to kiss me goodbye?"

When I picked up my bag again, she asked, "Where will you be staying in New York in case I need you?"

"Hotel Bedford. But why would you need me?"

"I just happened to think," she said. "That bullet came right between us. How do I know it was meant for you?"

It gave me something else to think about on the plane.

Seventeen

Buzz Bryant sounded worried when I called him from Kennedy Airport on Long Island. "No sign of Decker, not a word. We've only got three hours till game time. I'm calling the police in on it."

"Good idea. You do have another center?"

"Sure. We got Hollis. But he ain't Decker. No more than Decker is Gonzaga." He managed a derisive chuckle. "Unless he's as good in the sack as he thinks he is."

I remembered Decker's wistful yearnings and my tentative promise to apprise Joanna Burton he was on his way. "He didn't leave any word where he might be going?"

"One of the guys said he got a phone call. It didn't seem to worry him any. When he went out, he said he had to see somebody, or had something to do. Like that. He didn't explain. His roomie thought he might have added that it wouldn't take long."

"Who was that?"

"Robinson."

"I'm heading for the Bedford. I'll ask around and call you back."

The Bedford was one of the older small hotels off Fifth, boasting an authentic Victorian lounge and dining room, with no chi-chi, aging gracefully, serving good food and drink without forcing you into hock.

I checked in, had a quick shower and shave, grabbed something for the inner man, and snagged a cab for a downtown run. I directed him toward the East Side and 23rd Street and settled back on the worn leather.

The cabbie pushed his protective glass back an inch. "Who d'ya like t'night?"

"Lakers," I said.

"You gotta be from outta town," he said. "The Knicks will only wipe the floor wid 'em."

"Maybe," I said. "We took the first two. Remember?"

"Sure. But you had Gonzaga then. Right?"

"Right."

"So who you got now—that stewbum Hollis?"

"Hollis?" I sounded surprised. "What Hollis? Ellis Decker is the big man in the middle now."

The cabbie guffawed. "Don't bet on it. I heard he took a powder."

"You got to be kidding. Not Decker. It's his big chance."

"I know. I guess he knows it too. But he don't have heart, y'see. Friend of mine saw him grabbin' a cab yesterday. I hoid he didn't show up at practice this morning. Don't that signify somethin'? It means he ain't takin' no chances."

"What time did your friend see him go?"

"Around five. Well, am I right? How does it figger to you?"

"It doesn't," I said. "For Decker not to play tonight, he'd have to be dead."

The cabbie nodded and turned his wheel. "Well, yeah. Dat's possible too."

I paid him off at the corner of 23rd and added a tenner. "My name is Roper and I'm at the Bedford. If your friend sees Decker again any place, I'd like to hear about it."

The cabbie looked at the bill. "Okay. Only what if he don't see him?"

"Then you made yourself ten bucks."

"Okay, buddy. For your sake, I hope I can make the call."

I got out of his cab. "What do you mean—for *my* sake?"

He shrugged. "Anybody's got a piece of the Lakers t'night, I feel sorry for 'em."

He pulled away from the curb and I headed across the street. There was a light upstairs. The sign under it said:

110

MALACHI LEE'S SCHOOL OF ISSHINRYU KARATE
ARTFUL DEFENSE

I walked up the stairs, my footsteps covered by the sounds of stomping and bodies thudding to the floor. I opened the door to see my friend back-pedaling on a mat while a little wild-eyed girl came at him. She came to about Malachi's waist, advancing with side kick (yoko-geri), ankle kick (kansetsu-geri) and her fists.

The girl was about eleven, wearing the standard karate costume, pure and white, barefoot, as were the other tykes I saw watching in the studio. Malachi saw me, held his hand up, turned to me and bowed. The little girl kept on kicking. Malachi caught her foot casually, pulled and dumped her on her karateka keester.

"Think about that," he said softly and came off the mat to greet me.

"I'll wait," I said. "Maybe she'll throw you."

"She doesn't get another chance tonight. Class is over." He clapped his hands. The kids lined up, came to attention, and in turn stepped up to their instructor, bowing formally. It was part of the training and discipline, and Malachi drew himself up to his full six-seven and jackknifed at the waist repeatedly until they had all filed out.

His brochure listed him as an Afro-American, citizen of the United States. Holder of 4th-degree (Yo-Dan) Black Belt in Isshinryu Karate and 2nd-Degree (Ni-Dan) Black Belt in Nisei-Goju Karate.

Coming in at about two-twenty, he was an authentic heavyweight karate champion, black belt division, had won the title and successfully defended many times. When he wasn't knocking grown men over for fun, he was teaching children how to handle themselves. The bullies weren't kicking sand in people's faces any more, they had found other ways. Malachi was doing his own thing to give the nonbelligerents some protection, using his master plan of Artful Defense.

I had enlisted Malachi's services to help me stay alive and well in the pursuit of my duties. I didn't have the man's grace, the unconcerned ease with which he could deal out destruction, the balanced poise floating over the turmoil of action, I used what I had learned, and survived.

The mixed group of junior karatekas, back in street togs, went out and down the stairs.

Malachi showed me a chair. "I heard about Gonzaga. I was expecting you."

"Why here? Gonzaga was killed on the West Coast."

Malachi smiled. "I thought perhaps you wanted a quick refresher course."

"No way," I said. "My trouble is I'm too good at it. I had a little bout the other night in Nuevo Laredo. Used the three-on-one moves you gave me. The trouble was, I killed all three of them."

Malachi stared at my feet, then pointed to the sign on the wall. "It's supposed to be 'artful defense'—did you have to kill them?"

"Not *that* fast. I had some questions to ask first, dammit."

Malachi spread his hands open. "Then you wanted to kill them."

"I guess that's it," I admitted. "They were in on the Gonzaga killing from the beginning."

"I want to hear about it," he said.

I gave him the story from the start, when I was whipsawed in my own apartment. When I came to the eye-opening Belmont twiggie and her offensive about I AM-ness, Malachi smiled. "Does she have anything there?" I asked.

"That idea's been around a long time. Patanjali started it around the second or third century B.C. with his Yoga Sutras. He wasn't the founder of yoga but an important systemizer, representing a dualistic and ascetic attitude."

"Okay. Break it down for me. You're not as pretty as she is. Maybe I can concentrate better here."

"It stems from the ultimate identity crisis: Who am I? Maybe you could understand it better as a Zen enlightenment consisting of an immediate grasp of Being which is beyond the subject-object relationship of ordinary consciousness."

"Frankly, no," I said.

"It's a Self-to-Self relation, transcending thought, feeling and analysis. Happening on the level of awareness. True giving arises when one relates to another in this way."

Seeing my furrowed brow, Malachi tried one more time. "Think of it as the action without thought of the fruit of action." He gave me a moment for that, and added, "That's how it's recommended in the Bhagavad-Gita. You got it now?" He saw I didn't. "It depends on how angry or dissatisfied you are with yourself. When I am finally fed up and angry with my ego, I can finally part with my identification with it."

I held up my hand. "Okay. That's what she was talking about."

"Fine," Malachi said. "I know what she was talking about. I still can't say as much for you."

I gave him the rest of it, with Wu getting away, the call from the Laker coach Bryant on my return, all the way down to the cabbie on the street in the know about Ellis Decker running out. Despite his singular skill in kicking people loose from their skulls, Malachi is a mystery buff, and as knowledgeable as a man can be who walks around barefoot most of the time on his job. "It doesn't figure," he said. "Why would he run out? Tonight's his chance to prove he's his own man, just as Gonzaga was."

"That's the way I see it."

"Okay. So he didn't run out. Somebody persuaded him."

"There would have to be a gun at the other end of it."

Malachi spread his big hands. "We're both reasonably sure it wasn't your cabbie or his friend."

"Wu got away. I spoiled his action in Mexico. Could it be he headed East? Last I heard, the East Coast was awfully tight for dope smugglers."

"Maybe he thought it was time to open it up."

"He wanted Gonzaga and got him. I hit his joint, and he wants to get even and be top man. He nails Decker and makes me out a chump all over again."

"Maybe," Malachi said cautiously. "I thought I was listening closely. When did you prove he killed Gonzaga?"

I got to my feet. "I didn't. It's all I have on the record playing for me. What makes you think Wu didn't?"

"A lot of people didn't."

I went back to my room at the Bedford without a lead, hoping the cabbie would call back and give me something to work on. The phone rang and I picked it up.

"Hello. You Roper?"

I felt my hand tighten. I looked at it and it had become the familiar killer fist. I thought I knew who it was but went through the motions, anyway. "I'm Roper. Who's this?"

My caller chuckled softly. "Smart guy. We see how smart you feel tomorrow."

The cadence was strangely familiar, the rickshaw patois I remembered from another call. "Are you calling about Decker? Do you have Decker, Wu?" I shouted.

"Decker," he repeated, and chuckled again.

I heard a click and the phone went dead in my hands.

There was still two hours until game time at the Garden. The phone rang again and I jumped and snarled into it.

"Hello, this is Tom Boswell."

"Who?"

"You remember—the cabbie just drove you downtown a while ago. I just seen my friend I told you about, the guy who said Decker got into a cab—an' he told me somethin' screwy. Are you ready?"

"What?"

"Decker wasn't carryin' no bag on him." He waited a second, then added, "You get it?"

"Not yet. What?"

"Well, if he was takin' a powder like we figgered, then he'd take his bag with him, no? You don't check out widout your bag. So what I make out is this—he wasn't takin' no powder. You agree?"

"Sounds reasonable."

"Okay. So if you din't get your ten bucks' worth, it's the best I can do. Okay?"

"It's worth another ten-spot if your friend can remember where Decker was going. I'll leave it at the desk for you."

"You're a big sport. Hold it just a sec." I heard him yell off the phone and then another man's voice. "He says Decker got off at Fifth and 59th. He hurried across the street like he was gonna meet somebody in the park. Okay?"

"How does your friend know all this? Was he the driver of the cab?"

"Ya guessed it, sport. So it's the real McCoy. Okay?"

"Why didn't you tell me he was the driver, in the first place?"

"Be reasonable, Mac. If he comes down to talk about it, it costs him a day's pay. Why should I hurt the guy?"

"All right, Boswell. Do me another favor and ask your pal if he can pin down the exact time he let him out near the park. It might help."

He came back on in a minute. "He says it was five on the nose. He remembers first, because it was like a coincidence, see—Fifth Avenya at five. Second, because it's down in his book. Okay, you all square now?"

I called Buzz Bryant. He said the police were out looking. I phoned Malachi at his *dojo*. "A cabbie let Decker out at Fifth and 59th, across from the park, at five o'clock yesterday. What do you think?"

"I think I'll meet you there in fifteen minutes."

There was an outside chance Decker could have been mugged in the park after keeping his appointment. Malachi and I checked behind the big rocks and shrubbery at the park entrance, then went around the lake footpath. Night was closing in, the wind sharp and cold. There were a few solitary winos sleeping on the park benches, none of them basketball players.

We swung north, following the footpath leading to the zoo house. Malachi touched my arm. "I think we can stop looking."

A thin cordon of blue-coated cops fanned out from the open yard of a maintenance building off the elephant house. "What have you got in there?" I asked.

The beefiest one shrugged. "A body."

"We're looking for Ellis Decker."

"Maybe you can tell us if it's Decker."

The yard was covered by a thick matting of loose straw.

Enough of Decker's body had been visible for the fuzz searching the park area, and they had pulled him out and left him there until the medical examiner came along.

A pitchfork with long reddened prongs was lying alongside his stiff contorted body. Around his neck were the deep blue circular marks that a good strangling job with a wire coathanger leaves.

I hunkered over Decker, wondering if he realized at the moment the wire had pulled taut on his neck that he would never get the chance to show the world how good he was. By the time the pitchfork had been thrust into his chest, he probably would have forgotten all his dreams.

Malachi Lee stroked his chin and made like Holmes. "Whoever did this job brought him to the right place."

"How do you make that?"

"This is the zoo, man. He was an animal."

Eighteen

Camino looked at the fresh stick of gum in one hand and the unlit cigarette in the other. "Some day maybe I'll try chewing them both together. I could be missing something."

"If Wu was in New York, I never found him," I said. "If he's opening up some new connections there, the narc bureau doesn't know about it. The phone call to me could have been made direct, long distance. But he had to be there to kill Decker."

"Kind of a good trick for a little Oriental chubby man to strangle a seven-foot basketballer," Camino said. He picked a sheet of paper off his desk. "Oddly, you were right about him running drugs. I got this from Colonel Perales, the Commandant in Nuevo Laredo you loused up by busting in on Wu before they could nail him. They have him down as Frankie Wu. They figure he's smuggled over two hundred million dollars' worth of heroin into this country between January a year ago and May."

"Did they find out how he's getting it in?" The figure Camino gave represented street value of five hundred kilograms, enough heroin to supply the nation's entire addict population for three weeks.

"Hidden in cans of imported tea," Camino said. "In expensive cameras and stereo sets. In secret compartments of imported autos."

I shrugged. "They've got that much. Why didn't they nail him?"

"They were waiting to find out his American connection."

117

I thought of Belmont immediately but didn't want to get Camino irritated so early in the morning.

Camino put the gum and cigarette down and picked up a pipe. He packed it with tobacco, lit it up, drew the smoke down his throat and coughed. He put the pipe down. "Hell, I can get a cough with less trouble smoking a cigarette."

"Another crazy thing," I said, "was the Lakers winning last night without Decker. Hollis threw in thirty-six points all by himself and blocked twenty shots. Tell me what the hell Wu got out of that?"

"You already told me. A sore pitchfork." He picked up another paper, glanced at it quickly, then threw it down. "If you're right about Wu, you're wrong about his connection. Perales mentions another ring, two rings, actually. Shipped from Marseilles directly to Miami or New York, or else the dope goes on a roundabout route from Europe to South America to the U.S.—he calls that route 'the triangle of death.' You call yours the Golden Triangle."

"I like mine better. That whiz kid you sent me to at UCLA pegs Wu as Chinese. He's got to be the front man for his boss in Burma, Lo. When I get him, I'll prove it."

Camino indicated the pipe, tobacco pouch, gum stick, cigarette and lighter on his desk. "Wish I could help you, but you can see how busy I am. Rotsa ruck."

The Belmont twiggie called me when I got home.

"Did you kill anybody in New York?" she asked gaily.

"No."

"Was your head zonked?"

"No."

"Have you found out yet who was shooting at us?"

"No. Not that, either."

"Well, what have you been doing?"

"Getting an immediate grasp of Being which is beyond the subject-object relationship of ordinary consciousness."

"What?"

"Thinking of the action without thought of the fruit of action."

"I don't understand you. Are you drunk?"

"It's more of a Self-to-Self relation, transcending thought, feeling and analysis at the level of awareness."

"Are you sure you weren't zonked? You're sure talking funny."

"I'm a funny fellow. Have you seen your uncle whom you don't see any more lately?"

"Not since the last time. Why?"

"Do you happen to know what he has in those big crates in his warehouse?"

"No," she said. "Would you like me to ask him?"

I repressed a shudder. "No. Forget I mentioned it."

"When are you coming over to see one of my paintings?"

"As soon as I make a Chinese connection."

"I didn't know you liked chop suey. There's a keen place here at the marina."

"What's it called?"

"New Jade Palace." She giggled. "You know where it is?"

"Not yet."

"It's on Panay Way. Doesn't that sound romantic? That's the place where you got—"

"I never noticed it. Meet you there for lunch."

"You're kidding. When?"

"Twelve o'clock. Today."

"Wow! Remember, it's kind of a formal place—you have to wear shoes."

The shaggy-haired whiz kid with the perfect set of teeth answered the phone. I identified myself and asked if La Salle was there. She said no, he happened to be home with a cold.

"He said you were wrong about your tape reading. Has he convinced you yet that your deduction was wrong?"

"Listen, Mr. Roper, if I'm wrong, I'll eat that tape."

"You would have to find it first, I suppose."

"I can't believe that, either. Why would anybody want to steal a tape from this office? It never happened before."

"Crime is a dirty game, Miss Shaw. Killing sometimes leads to stealing."

"Groovy. If you kill my boss, I'll let you steal me."

"It's worth the effort. Are you still brushing your teeth?"

"Yes."

"Good. Try to hang on."

"Thanks. Incidentally, you may think I'm crazy, but I could swear I heard a man speaking the other night whose voice was practically identical to your subject on the tape."

"All right. You're crazy. When was this?"

"Night before last."

"Where?"

"That new Chinese place at the marina—New Jade Palace."

"Did you happen to see the gentleman?"

"No. He was sitting at a booth behind me. I managed to get up a little later to check, just out of curiosity, but he was gone."

"That's the way it goes sometimes, Miss Shaw. When you want them, they're gone."

"If I come across him again, what do you think I should do?"

"It's elementary, Miss Shaw. Ask him where he was born."

The New Jade Palace tried hard but wasn't nearly as attractive as the girl in the booth. She was wearing shoes but not too much of anything else.

"Why are you looking around?" she asked. "I thought I was supposed to be your date. Are you expecting somebody else?"

"Just looking," I said. "I wasn't expecting him, but I was hoping to see a little fat Chinese gentleman with black hair and a modified Fu Manchu mustache."

"Oh, he was here," the girl said. "He was sitting right over there at the bar. He left just as you came in."

There was a side door a few steps from the bar. There was a service door leading to the kitchen. What there wasn't, was the little man so large in my fantasies called Frankie Wu.

Nineteen

I called a fellow I knew who happened to be in the seamier side of the business. He remembered me and a large favor I had done him when I prevented an aware and spied-on spouse from blasting him away from his listening devices with a shotgun.

"Ask and you got it," he said. "Anything you want. Except a tape I rolled last night. It would spoil you forever and make you hate girls."

"I don't want it, Mel. I'm wondering if you might have handled a case a few years back before they put through the easier divorce law."

"All I need is a couple names," he said. "It helps me think."

I gave him the name and it struck a spark immediately. "Sure, I remember that sonofabitch. His wife was a living doll, believe me. He was two-timing her, with another guy yet. It was a pleasure to nail him with the evidence."

"Thanks. Did she get married again?"

"I don't think so. I guess it'll take her a while to get over this louse. Lucille's still in town, incidentally, in case you want more of the story from her. I bumped into her last week at the supermarket."

"What were you doing at the supermarket?"

"The manager's wife is suspicious about some lady who's been buying an awful lot of groceries every day."

"Thanks, pal. I guess we're even now."

"Are you kidding? We were even a long time ago. I only keep feeding you this stuff because I know you don't have the guts to do it yourself. You'd rather punch a guy's head off or kill him."

"To each his own. Mel baby, I love you."

"Say it again so I can get it on tape."

She was slim and lovely, blond and a little tipsy. She lived in a good neighborhood where they didn't allow house-to-house canvassing, piano playing or race riots.

"Mrs. Lucille La Salle?"

"I guess. Who the hell are you?"

I showed her my buzzer. She started to shake her head. "No, thanks, I already had one." Then she heard the rest of it and smiled, opening the door wider. "Walk right in."

She made it across the room with an undulating hip sway that made me a little nervous, sensing her vulnerability and my own. She came back splashing a lot of booze into a big glass, pushed me down on the sofa with one hand and sank into a soft chair opposite me, showing a lot of leg, every inch of it smooth-looking and symmetrical.

"What do you wanna know about the sonofabitch?"

"I already have a pretty good idea why he hates private eyes. Just a little of the background would help."

She took a good long belt. "You're looking at part of the background right now, y'know. I wasn't a lush until I met Larry boy. Well, actually, not till mush—much later. We met up in Berkeley, went to college together. He was a serious kid, a grind, didn't seem to be able to hack it with girls. I felt sorry for the sonofabitch, started dating him, and before I knew it, for Crissakes, I let him knock me up and we got married."

I looked around for pictures, without seeing any.

She shook her blond head. "No. No baby. He got scared and I got rid of it. My folks had money and found me a good doc. After we got married they kept supporting us, got us the house and trimmings. I got a job and supported Larry boy while he flunked his bar exam and had to start another line—that voice line, whatever the hell it's called.

"He got very interested in his work, stopped coming home nights, I got a bit suspicious, hired your friend, and whaddaya know—it was another gay boy he was dating. Would you believe it?"

I remembered La Salle nuzzling his shaggy-haired helper. "Sometimes they swing both ways."

"That's what I hear," she said mockingly.

"It could be his background," I said cautiously. "Maybe he felt the need of a sophisticated life style."

"Sophisticated, my foot! He was a farm boy right out of Georgia. A hick all the way through college, and after. He may act like a big shot now up at the college, with all that voice-print computer double-talk, but one will get you five he's still a hick, as well as a sonofabitch."

I had all I needed now, and got off the sofa. "If it's any comfort to you, you're not alone in that opinion."

She walked me to the door. "Try me again sometime when I'm sober. I might make a better impression."

"I'm impressed now. But I have to make a few more house calls."

"That's the idea," she said. "Spread it around. Heal the sick."

The husky blond crew-cut behind the desk in the security office at Los Angeles airport knew me. He flipped a hand toward the metal-detector box the hijacking craze had brought into being. "Stay away from that thing," he cracked. "It might pick up your steel nerves and start buzzing. I'd have to take you off the plane."

"I made my trip already. I was wondering how good that gimmick is so far as really stopping anybody."

He indicated the counter and shelves behind him. It was a madman's arsenal of hunting knives, kitchen knives, stilettos, curved daggers, hatchets, long-bladed razors, sharpened belt buckles and brass knuckles. There were handguns of every size and description, sawed-off shotguns, submachine guns and target pistols. I didn't see any bazookas, howitzers, grenade-launchers or cannons, pointing out this discrepancy to my colleague in crime prevention.

He laughed. "Some people don't try hard enough. They got the idea we can spot anything."

He showed me another counter littered with trusses, corsets, bras with metal fasteners, sword canes, hatpins and silver pillboxes.

"We usually find these in the rest rooms. You'd be surprised how many people hate the idea of embarrassment. They'll dump anything rather than set the alarm buzzer off."

"What if my great-aunt is running heroin in her girdle?"

"She'll have to leave the heroin. We give her back her girdle."

"Suppose you think it's heroin but it's only aspirin."

"She still gets her girdle back. If it's aspirin, we send her a new bottle. We take names and addresses on all suspects. We have to make good or they'd sue us."

I asked to see his week's list. There wasn't any name I recognized except my own. I looked at a lot of flight time schedules and checked the advance reservation listing. If Frankie Wu was going someplace, he didn't know it yet or he had a better way of going.

Twenty

I drove back to town again, thinking about Gonzaga and the
killer outside who had waited patiently in the night, cool and
confident of his skill.

I imagined Decker's killer had to be cool and confident too.
Decker was no Gonzaga, but he was close to seven feet, bigger
than most men. A young giant, a powerful athlete, with big
hands, good reflexes.

His killer hadn't been afraid to work at close quarters. That
implied a lot of assurance.

A red light stopped me at a busy corner. Across the street,
people were standing in a long double line on the sidewalk. They
shuffled slowly along, stopping at the box-office window to
purchase admittance tickets. Business at the Gin and Gaslight
Club looked good on this Saturday night.

I still had questions to ask the blond songstress Joanna
Burton. A few concerned her wealthy and eccentric ex—Jules
Belmont. I remembered her telling me that on Sunday, her day
off, she would have time to see me.

It had all started on the previous Sunday. I was running a
losing race and impatient to break out of it. A few answers
tonight, a few facts might break the puzzle open for me.

I found a parking place around the corner from the club.
From the rear, I could hear the throbbing beat of rock music, a

bleating voice raised in song. A burst of applause. It was hard to realize people were out for the night enjoying themselves.

The doorman noticed I had by-passed the box-office line. He waved me back, indicating I needed a ticket to get in. I asked him first what time Joanna Burton went on.

He shook his bushy head. "She ain't on tonight, buddy." Her name was on the wall placard, featured as an additional attraction under the larger type that spelled out JOE COOLIDGE. When I pointed this out, the doorman shook me another negative. "I know, I know. But she ain't working tonight."

"Is she ill?" I asked.

"I don't know, pal. She didn't make it last night, either."

"Anybody here know why?"

"Try her agent. Maybe he knows."

"What's his name?"

"Beats me. Ask Joanna."

She didn't answer the number she had written down for me, but I still had her address. It was in West Hollywood just below the hills. I wheeled around the last corner and found the number of her house. It was past Doheny on a small side street that wound up in a dead end, giving the few homeowners here all the privacy they wanted.

The lights were out. I tried the door, the knocker and the bell. That didn't bring any response, either. The curtains were drawn. I went around the side. She didn't have her car parked there. I didn't know if she had a car, but nobody gets by in this town without one.

The high fence at the side gave me some of the owner's privacy and I went in through the French doors. They were locked but made of old wood and I jiggled them around and forced them apart.

The living room was dark. I found a light, and nobody called out "Who's there?" when I flicked it on. It was a nice living room, feminine, with good furniture and accessory decorations. There were paintings on the walls but I didn't have time to appraise them.

I found Joanna Burton upstairs, sprawled across her king-sized bed, looking a lot worse than the last time I'd seen her. She wasn't wearing very much and most of that had been torn off. She hadn't been strangled and there weren't any ice picks in her ears, but taken all in all, her murderer had demonstrated he was no slouch when it came to killing.

Her head had been battered, her face punched out of shape, her body slashed, stabbed and butchered. Unless the killer had carelessly nicked his little finger, all the blood had to be hers.

She was cold and stiff and she wouldn't have to worry any more about second billing. The drawers of her dressers had been pulled out, her undies, stockings and other wearables strewn about, festooning the dressers like hanging wreaths on a gala holiday. I couldn't tell what the killer was looking for, or if he had found it. I could only marvel at the energy he had left after doing all that good work on the girl.

I called Camino. He wasn't in his office. I fixed myself a drink and waited for him to call me back. He took his time and I had a few more drinks and looked around. If there were any clues indicating somebody in her life who took offense easily, I failed to notice them.

I gave it all to Camino when he finally called. He asked, "Where does that leave you now?"

"It's finished now," I told him. "She's number three."

"What the hell does that mean?"

"That's as far as it goes. The next one is on me."

"Okay. Call me back when you're sober."

"They come in threes," I told him. "It's the killing cycle. I even told that to Power."

"Who?"

"Tom Power. The Forum security guard. Used to play for the Lakers. Bum knee."

"That the guy used to drink a lot Gonzaga was always bailing out?"

"That's right. But he's got that problem licked now."

"I'm glad to hear it," Camino said. "Because now he's got a different kind of problem."

"Like what?"

"He's got two kids—they were just being brought in, going to be busted for possession."

"How old?"

"Fourteen—sixteen. What else?"

"Hard stuff?"

"Marijuana."

"That's all he needs to go on a real tear. See what you can do meanwhile, Nick. I'm coming down."

They were young and tough. If they were scared, they didn't show it. They had the hard look of hate you see on the kids today.

"My name is Roper," I told them. "I know your dad. Maybe I can help."

The younger one spit at my shoes. "Shove it."

I turned to the older boy. "This your first offense?"

He showed me his thumb. "Up yours!"

I looked at Camino.

"Rotsa ruck," he said.

"Go ahead," said the younger one. "Call the old man. We couldn't care less. Neither would he give a damn."

"That's if you can find him," the older boy said, jeering. "He left home."

"When was this?" I asked.

When they looked stubbornly at me without answering, Camino said "Excuse me" and stepped between us. He grabbed one stubborn head in each of his big hands and brought them together. "Mr. Roper asked you boys a question and he'd like an answer. He happens to be a friend of the family, you see."

"A week ago," they said.

"Any particular reason?" I asked.

They smirked. "He's got the hots for some dame," the younger one said.

"It's not the first time," the older one added.

"Now how would you know that?" Camino asked. "Does he tell you boys when he has the 'hots' for a dame?"

"He don't have to," the older one said. "We can tell."

"How?" I asked.

They looked at each other and made their own silent signals. The older one carried the ball. "He took us to the Forum one night to see the Lakers. He can get the free tickets when he wants, you know. After the game he took us back to see the guys. You know, like Jerry and Gail and Jo-Jo Gonzaga. That's how we know."

Camino and I exchanged our own signals for being mystified. "How was that?" Camino asked.

"Gonzaga had some doll waiting for him. The old man looked at her and you could tell he flipped."

Camino stayed with it. "How could you tell he flipped?"

"He got red in the face, and got all sweaty."

Camino looked tired and disgusted. "No wonder you kids got picked up for holding. You're dumb, that's why. I don't need any doll to get me red in the face and make me sweaty. I'm probably doing it right now talking to little jerks like you."

"You're doing it," I said. "Maybe they have another way of knowing Power flipped."

"He carries her picture in his wallet," the younger one offered.

"How would you know that?" Camino asked. "Did he show it to you?"

"We needed to borrow some money," the kid said. "He works nights at the Forum and sleeps in the daytime. He had his pants hung on a chair."

"That's nice," Camino said softly.

"Maybe you can remember," I said, "if she had blond hair."

"No. It was black," he said. "Long and black."

I shrugged off Camino's questioning stare. "Gonzaga had a great many ladies, remember. The Burton girl might have thought she was something special to him, but Jo-Jo had his own life style."

"In a kind of way," the older boy said suddenly, "I don't blame the old man. She sure was stacked."

Camino turned abruptly to the desk sergeant. "Do you mind?" he asked.

The desk man smiled affably. "Be my guest. I got a couple of my own."

Power's young hard ones began to look nervous when Camino came back to them rubbing his big hands. "Well, boys," he said softly, "I learned a little about you two tonight. I know you smoke a little pot, do a little spying, and steal from your old man when he's asleep. All I want to know is one more thing. Can you run?"

The boys looked at each other, then back at him. "Run?"

Camino pointed over their shoulders. "There's the door," he roared suddenly. "Now go on and get out of here! Beat it! If you're not gone in three seconds, I'm throwing the book at you."

They both showed good early foot and took the turn well. When they were gone, Camino let the remaining air out of his deep chest. "Sorry I brought you down. Maybe you were better off doing what you were doing—getting drunk."

"No problem," I told him. "I remember where I was when I left off."

"Come on," he said gently. "We all got problems. You can't win 'em all. Just tell me something. Do you figure Frankie Wu for the Burton job too?"

"That's what I'm going to find out right now," I said.

Twenty-one

The low white line of concrete blocks Jules Belmont had stacked together for his enterprises in El Segundo didn't show any lights. A couple of big trucks were parked on the ramp outside the closed warehouse door. Three cars were parked above them, side by side. One was a ten-year-old Chevy Impala that had to have 100,000 miles on it. The original gray paint had faded, the fenders and sides had dents, and the tires had more prayers than rubber going for them. The second was a glistening black Cad sedan. The third was a little pink VW with a canvas-top roof.

There wasn't any visible night shift working the plant. I came around the side and cut to the rear of the building. The rear door was locked but I took care of that with my anti-burglar-proof key. I went tippie-toe down the long dark corridor. Belmont's office door was closed. A rim of light leaked through the bottom. I heard voices and I turned the doorknob and went in.

There were three of them in the room, behind the desk. Belmont was on the left, looking older and more worried than his gray sweater. The hip and very lovely I AM-ness kid, his niece, sat at the center holding the phone. On the right side was a plump little man with slick black hair, black alert eyes, a straggly black mustache. He had something in his hand that was just as black and twice as menacing. It looked like a Mauser Automatic Pistol, the .32 caliber, the big baby. It holds nine shots and is guaranteed to shoot in a six-inch circle at twenty-five yards, in a two-inch circle at ten. It was pointed at the Belmont twiggie's head, and I put mine down.

The dark-haired girl stared at me open-mouthed without losing any appeal. It's no easy trick but she had more. She tapped the phone in her hand. "Incredible!" she said. "We were just trying to call you at your place." She let the phone drop into its cradle. She indicated the little Chinese man on her left with a tentative gesture constrained slightly by the gun in her ear. "You're in luck! Isn't this the gentleman you weren't really expecting but hoped would be there the other afternoon at the New Jade Palace? The one I said left the bar almost the moment you walked in?"

"He is, indeed, Miss Belmont. Incredible is the word, all right." I looked at the little man who was trying to carry on where Fu Manchu left off. "Frankie Wu?"

Without the gun, he didn't look any more dangerous than a misspelled fortune cookie. But he had it, and he wigwagged it now, nodding at mine, then the desk, his Mauser still in the girl's ear.

I made as if to toss it to him, but apparently he had heard of that one, and shook his head slightly, smiling and bending the girl's ear a trifle more at the same time.

I shrugged, walked over and put it on the desk. He nodded politely. "She doesn't have good sense, Wu, but she does have good hearing. She could probably hear your gun go off even if you held it a foot away."

He favored me with another fleeting smile and withdrew the Mauser a few inches. "You Roper," he said in impeccable pidgin English, "what you doing here?"

His voice had the same singsong lilt I remembered. It felt good to know I was right, but that wasn't good enough to go around now. Belmont hadn't spoken yet. We had a pretty select group and it seemed only fair to include him in the conversation.

"His ex-wife was murdered. I just found her body."

Belmont managed a word. "Joanna?"

"The very same," I said. "Not that she looked it, any more. Whoever killed her is without a doubt the top man around in bloodletting." I bowed slightly to Wu. "Sorry, Frankie, but even including you."

"I never killed your friend Gonzaga," he said.

"I know," I said. "It was two other fellows."

The Belmont girl was leaning back stiffly in her uncle's swivel chair trying to get her head away from Wu's gun. She went back too far, lost her balance, screamed, yanking the phone and its cradle base along with her as she toppled over.

She made a pretty picture, her long lovely legs flashing, her short skirt showing more skin. Wu stepped back, grinning, enjoying the view. I knew there weren't any better around but work came first.

I came in blind-siding Wu with a snapping ankle kick (kansetsu-geri), catching him at the back of his right knee. His knee folded in, as it had to, and his arms went back to maintain his balance. His right hand holding the Mauser was closer and I chopped savagely at his wrist. The bone snapped and he cried out in pain, dropping the gun.

I added knife-hand strike to the collarbone (shuto sakotsu-uchi), and something went there, too, and he uttered another shrill cry. I gave him fore-fist strike to the chin (seiken ago-uchi), which is very much like a punch on the jaw. He fell back against the wall, and I grabbed him before he slid to the floor and dumped him down in a chair.

I got my gun back, kicked his aside, and was slapping him awake when the Belmont twiggie came up from behind the desk muttering what sounded like a few choice obscene phrases.

She threw the phone back on her uncle's desk, got her chair straight, and then suddenly realized something was missing— the gun in her ear. She looked around for it, took in the new scene with me slapping Wu awake, and her eyes opened wider.

"I missed it all, dammit," she said. "I don't suppose you would do that all over again?"

Private eyes are notoriously terse; I grunted, fulfilling my obligations. Wu was moaning, eyelids closed and fluttering, trying to cover his broken wrist and collarbone with his good arm. I wanted to tell him that for a man so fragile, he ought to have picked another line. Belmont hadn't moved a muscle. He sat slumped in the other chair, his arms folded around his stomach as if an ulcer had been telling him something he had heard before.

"You told me last time," I said, "that you gave up Joanna because she was too expensive. Maybe now that she's dead, you can come up with a better reason."

His hooded eyes regarded me without expression. He glanced sideways at his niece. She didn't do any more for him. "You know why," he said slowly. "It doesn't take too much to guess why." He had the picture on his right and he took it off the shelf and looked down at the glass. "You saw what she looked like. I wouldn't be surprised if you liked what you saw. A lot of men did."

"And Joanna liked that?"

Belmont snorted in reply.

"Okay. Was she fooling around? Playing the field or one man in particular."

"There was one gave her a lot of his time and attention. A big guy. Joanna always liked them big."

I remembered a pretty big one. "Was it Gonzaga?"

Belmont shook his head. "No."

"Can you remember his name?"

Belmont curled his thin lip and hugged himself tighter. "What the hell difference does it make?" he croaked. "After him, there was another, and after him, probably somebody else. There was probably somebody before him, and a long line of them before that." He grunted. "You don't want a name, you want a memory bank."

"Okay," I said. "You had a reason. Do you intend springing for her funeral?"

"What the hell for? Do I look that generous?"

"Frankly, no, Mr. Belmont. You don't."

Belmont grinned crookedly and jutted his chin in the direction of his niece. "Ask Barbara. She can tell you how I am about money. She knows a lot about me."

"I've a feeling that tonight she knows a little more." I looked at the girl; it didn't stimulate her. Wu moaned again. I got his tie off and handed it to her. "Make a sling around his neck for his wrist." She obeyed with no fuss and I waved her off. "We've got to be good to the bad guys. Now what's *your* story, Miss Belmont? What are you doing here tonight?"

"That's a silly question," she snapped. "I did it for you."

Before I could ask what that might be, she added, "You asked me what my uncle had in those big crates in his warehouse, didn't you? And you didn't want me to ask him, either. So I came over tonight to take a look for myself."

"Crazy," I said. "What did you find?"

"I found Uncle Jules—and this man here—didn't want visitors."

"Don't feel bad. It was a good try." I turned to Belmont. "Remember I asked you about a Chinese gentleman? You didn't remember any."

Belmont's face was too blue to blanch easily. "Who the hell are you to ask me questions? My business is my own business."

"You knew about a few other things than your own business. You sent your niece to your boat to pick up some party masks. You knew what kind of party masks they were, didn't you?"

"I had a rough idea," Belmont admitted. "Mr. Wu told me about how he protected the identity of his men when they picked you up. I didn't want anything turning up later."

"Which brings me to an interesting point. What was that all about?"

"Ask Wu," Belmont said testily. "He's awake now."

He was sitting back in the chair, his face grimacing with pain, no longer the placid unemotional type. He saw my gun fixed on his Chinese short-ribs.

"Okay, Roper," he said. "You pretty good."

"Plenty good," I said. "This gun plenty good, too. You were telling me before, you didn't kill Gonzaga."

"No way," he said.

"None of your men? Maybe you had another guy with a long-range rifle lined up and you forgot to call him off."

"No way," he repeated. "It was all a bluff. We never meant to kill him any time."

"I'm only going by what you told me," I said. "You told me on the boat that if Gonzaga played, he'd be dead. You said I'd be just as dead. Gonzaga played, and the second night he was dead. How come I'm still around?"

"Maybe you just plain lucky. Anyway, we tried a bluff. Nobody was going to kill anybody."

"Okay. Why the bluff?"

Wu's eyes flicked across to Belmont. "I needed a favor. To get the favor, I had to do Belmont a favor. You get it?"

"Not so far." I remembered Benny the Runner and his rumor. I had to hope Belmont would confirm it. "Were you heavy on the games?"

"Suppose I was?"

"Then you had to know you stood a better chance of getting it back if Gonzaga was out of it. I know you were down for a heap. Trying to bluff Gonzaga out of playing figures. What I don't get so far is how I came into it. You didn't know me. Frankie Wu didn't know me. I'm not that close to Gonzaga. How the hell did I get roped into it?"

Wu coughed, and then made himself smile a little. "You remember Santos? Pablo Santos?"

"Sure he's the Mexican gentleman who had a pretty good narc ring going in Acapulco until I busted it up a few years back."

"Okay. You remember him and so also he remember you. Okay?"

"Fair is fair," I said agreeably.

Wu rubbed his shoulder and winced. "This damn racket only doing one damn favor after another. I needed help from Santos. He said okay. When you get up there to L.A. you make it up to me, you take care of this Roper. Okay? So we smeared you around a little. If you talk Gonzaga out of playing, maybe we let a little more talk out. You responsible. Makes you chicken. All part of same favor, see?"

"I dig. And the other favor you do for Belmont here was so he would do *you* a favor—push your stuff around to some of his markets."

"No say," Wu said firmly.

"Okay, no say. We find out pretty dam' quick. Now what about Decker?"

Wu looked as innocent as a fortune cookie without its little slip of fortune paper. "Who Decker?"

"Gonzaga's replacement. He got himself killed back in New York two nights ago."

Wu shrugged with one shoulder. "Too bad. I been up here since you busted me in Nuevo Laredo."

"I hope you can prove it," I said. "Incidentally, you throw a pretty good knife. Melendez is dead."

"Melendez?"

"Your gate guard. He worked for Perales, the Police Commandant down there."

"Tough," Wu said. "A plant, huh? His bad luck. Say, you got any more questions? This arm hurts. Maybe I see about a doctor."

"I was saving the best one for last, Frankie. Where were you born?"

"Huh?"

"Birthplace. Country of origin. Before you drifted over to work for Lo."

He cocked his head. "Say, you know all that, too? You smart boy, Roper. Maybe you too smart, eh?"

"Never," I said firmly. "You never can be too smart for this racket. Look at the people I have to deal with. Now, once for the West Coast, Frankie. Where born?"

"Yunnan," he said. "Southern province of China."

I raised my hand in a mock salute. "Let's hear it for the little girl who eats the right kind of toothpaste."

The Belmont girl looked at me disapprovingly. "This is all too unreal. If you don't need me any more, I think I'll split this scene."

There was a commotion outside the door and five hundred battering rams suddenly assaulted Belmont's warehouse door. Camino came in with a lot of other fuzz. "You okay?" he asked. "We had you tailed just in case you knew what you were doing."

I beckoned the Belmont kid across the room. "We were just leaving. Say hello to Frankie Wu. He says he didn't kill anybody."

Camino nodded, looking unconvinced. "He has a memory block, maybe. Colonel Perales has him down for the agent Melendez, the ranch owner Rosales and about a dozen unconfirmed others, drug operators in the Nuevo Laredo district.

That's outside my beat, but a Federal grand jury here would be interested in what Mr. Wu's been bringing into this country."

"Mr. Belmont does a lot of business with him. Maybe he can tell you."

Belmont sat stiffly, arms folded across his body. His face looked bluer than ever and his hooded eyes didn't show a spark of friendship. "Go to hell," he croaked.

I took his niece's arm. It was warm and unresisting. "He's got a big warehouse," I told Camino. "Look around."

Camino glared, watching me cut toward the door. "I'm Homicide," he told me, "not Drugs. What the hell are you trying to suck me into?"

"A promotion," I said. "Find what they're bringing in and it'll be a feather in your cap."

"I don't need feathers," Camino growled. "I got you."

Twenty-two

La Salle liked his surroundings peaceful and quiet. He lived aloof from the pack in a little house on a hill overlooking Beverly Glen. The canyon was rustic and living in it not too expensive. Artists lived there, professors and angry guitar players. Deer roamed the hills, and sometimes a rattler would turn up or an occasional skunk. If the skunk had a friend, it would have to be La Salle.

At the corner of the narrow curving canyon road was a gas station. The phone booth was outside and commanded a view of Chrysanthemum Lane, which La Salle had to be fated to live on.

The number of Miss Shaw, the little girl with the perfect teeth and intuition to match, was in the directory. I called her and found her home. It was Saturday night and she should have been out with a guy, dancing and romancing. She knew that and so did I, but somehow the rest of the world wasn't in on it. I explained a favor I needed from her. She heard me out and didn't try to parlay it into a date.

I asked her if her boss was still at home with his cold. She knew it for a fact, as she had spoken to him only a short while ago.

"He hasn't been the same since your tape was stolen," she said. "I think it's got him down. To think that someone would do such a thing!"

"I know a way to get him up and restore his faith in

humanity. If you do what I ask, I guarantee you'll see results."

"Just open the window and throw things around?"

"That's the idea. Mess up the place. And when he gets there, keep him until I arrive."

"It sounds awfully mysterious," she said.

"I know. That's the only way I can do things."

She gave me his number before setting out, and I called. I was careful because I knew reading voices was La Salle's line. I made out I was one of the security guards patrolling the UCLA campus, a fellow I guessed could be Mahoney.

Mahoney sounded tough and Irish enough to suit me, and I hoped La Salle too. "We found your lab window open, Doc. It looks like somebody broke in. A lot of tapes on the floor and we got a hunch somebody's been at your computer. Maybe you oughtta get right down here."

The computer was closer to La Salle's heart than his navel. In a few minutes he came tearing down the hill wearing a shocking-pink Datsun sports car, zipped across the road and headed south for the college in Westwood.

His house had an inclined sundeck, a raised living room and a sunken garage. The garage had an inner door leading upstairs. I conned the lock with a plastic credit card and a bruised right shoulder and it let me in.

His kitchen was small, mod and streamlined for efficiency. You could reach for an egg, cook it and rinse the dish without leaving your chair. The refrigerator didn't have anything more mysterious in it than fresh food.

The living room had good Scandinavian furniture and a llama rug in front of a fieldstone fireplace. There were prints on the wall, books in the bookcase, current mags in the magazine rack. I wished I was as up-to-date as La Salle, and found the bedroom.

The bed was large and king-sized and there weren't any bodies in it, living or dead. It was a small comfort, but I was greedy and wanted more. Across the room was a big stereo set with all the hi-fi and recording gizmos. With that kind of equipment, there had to be tapes, and I found the lower shelf crammed with them. They were filed and stacked neatly. Some of them were for home entertainment, but there were a few questionables as well. A lot depended on whom you were hoping to entertain.

I found what I wanted, perhaps more than I had a right to expect. The next item was more difficult to locate. It had to be somewhere handy and yet not within casual sight. A boot under his bed had it deftly hidden. It had been cleaned carefully but used. I took that along too.

I flashed my buzzer for the young gate guard, told him where I was heading. "They came in a while ago," he said, and waved me through.

La Salle was walking around the lab room, a scarf around his throat, holding his head and muttering. The Shaw girl had taken advantage of the favor I had asked, and was wearing something short and filmy. I watched her swish around and kick things. She was making it more difficult to concentrate on what I had in mind, but I gritted the old teeth and knocked on the door from the inside.

La Salle saw me and scowled. "What the hell are you doing here?"

I threw open my hands and looked puzzled. "Beats me. Your security guard Mahoney called me. Said somebody had broken into your lab and I ought to get down here."

"He's got no authority to call you here," La Salle said angrily. "He's going to be out of a job when I get through with him."

"What happened here, Miss Shaw?" I asked, ignoring him.

"Oh, hello, Mr. Roper. It looks as if somebody broke in. That same guard Mahoney called me too."

La Salle stalked over to his desk, picked up a campus number-listing book and started snapping the pages. "I'm calling that sonofabitch right now and chew his ass out. He's got some explaining to do. I don't see a goddam thing missing."

"Hold it!" I barked. "I see something."

La Salle looked up, annoyed. "What the hell are you talking about?"

I stooped over the cabinet at the other end of the room, and when I got up, had it in my hand. "This," I said. It was one of my better performances, although La Salle wouldn't know that yet. "Well, I'll be damned!" I said, surprised.

"What is it?" asked the jiggling junior computer of the firm.

"This tape—wait a sec—there's a couple of them here. I guess they fell behind the others."

La Salle sneered. "So what, bright boy? We're looking for something that's supposed to be *missing*."

"That's right," I said. "That's what I found. This is the tape I brought in to you last week. Remember? The one you told me had been stolen."

La Salle was a better actor than I was, without trying. He registered honest surprise immediately and put more into it. "Why, that's impossible—I looked everywhere, I tell you!"

I had the spool out of its box and was examining it close to my eyes.

Miss Shaw asked, "What are you looking for?"

"To see if it's the same tape. The mystery man from China."

She took it from me, laughing. "There's an easier and better way to find out. We put it on the turntable and we play it."

"Great!" I said, smiling. La Salle looked glum, and I tried cheering him. "Isn't that a break? I told you that I thought it wasn't stolen—only misplaced."

The tape started spinning.

Hello. You Roper? Hello . . . You Roper? Hello . . . Hello . . . Roper . . . Roper . . . Hello, you Roper? Hello . . .

Miss Shaw looked at me, puzzled. "That's not it . . . I don't understand."

I shrugged. "Let it run a little more. Maybe it'll tell us something. Okay, La Salle?"

La Salle regarded me without warmth. He nodded coolly.

The tape went back to spinning. The Chinese accent was there, the same singsong pattern.

Hello . . . you Roper. Smart guy . . . smart guy . . . we see how smart . . . we see how smart . . . we see how smart you feel . . . you feel . . . feel . . . tomorrow . . . we see how smart you feel tomorrow . . .

Miss Shaw turned it off. "I don't get it."

I had the other tape in my hand. "Try this one. I must have given you the wrong one . . . I don't get it, either . . ."

She got it started and spinning. *Hello. You Roper? . . . Yes . . . this is Roper . . . How did you like the game? . . . Smart guy. We let this one go. We see how smart you feel tomorrow . . .* How about Gonzaga? Is he going to feel smart, too? . . . (a soft chuckle) *Gonzaga bigger fool than you. He not gonna feel anything because he gonna be pretty quick dead . . .*

Miss Shaw clapped her hands. "That's it! That's the one." She looked again at the preliminary tape. "But this one . . . Where did you find it?"

I gave her the old private eye's best offensive weapon, the shrug. "I don't recall offhand . . . there were three of them."

"Three?"

I had the last one in my hand. "Try this one for laughs."

La Salle stood stiffly, scarf tight around his throat, not objecting, sweating a lot, as they do with running fevers.

Hello. You Roper? . . . I'm Roper. Who's this? . . . (a soft chuckle) *Smart guy . . . we see how smart you feel tomorrow . . .* Are you calling about Decker? Do you have Decker, Wu? . . . *Decker* (another soft chuckle) . . .

I switched it off. "What do you think, La Salle?"

He wasn't thinking. His face glistened with sweat.

"You're the expert, La Salle. Did the same Chinese gentleman caller cut all three tapes?"

He gulped a little, remained silent and stayed with sweating. A slight shiver ran down his frame.

The Shaw kid cut in. "But it's so obvious, Dr. La Salle. Surely you can detect the difference?"

"Tell me," I said. "I'm new to this game."

"The second tape was the real one, of course. The man from Yunnan Province. The other two were fakes . . . Dr. La Salle could tell you that if he wasn't so ill . . ."

"I'm certain he could tell even more, Miss Shaw," I said affably. "You say two tapes were faked. Not made by the man from Yunnan?"

"Well," she said shyly, "the voice impersonation was really excellent. He probably has a very keen ear. But as I mentioned at your first visit, people really can't disguise their generic and regional origins and influences. Whoever made those fake recordings probably never came any closer to China than the New Jade Palace." She looked up at me hopefully and suggestively. "That's that Chinese restaurant at Marina del Rey."

"I've heard of it. At a rough guess, where would you say the impersonator hails from?"

"Somewhere between Kentucky and Georgia. If I had to pick one, it would be Georgia. That's Georgia, U.S.A., and not Russia. It's difficult to judge exactly off those tapes where he was speaking in a simulated dialect, not naturally."

I asked La Salle if he cared to comment, and it was clear he did not. "It's very odd," I said. "I was speaking to the former Mrs. La Salle not too long ago. She happened to mention, too, that you were from Georgia."

"But I didn't say—" the shaggy-haired girl started to say before clapping her hand to her mouth.

"That's the way these mysteries turn out," I told her. "One never knows. Dr. La Salle doesn't like private investigators, for reasons known best to himself alone, and a few fortunate others. He thought it would be fun to confuse me."

His pale moon face was paler. The Omar Sharif eyes lacked focus. He looked like a sick man becoming worse.

"It wasn't too hard confusing me," I continued, "because I was already confused from the beginning of this case. In fact, I might have still been confused if you hadn't been kind enough to save the evidence for me yourself. As an old crime investigator, I've got to give you a solid no-no on that, La Salle. Self-incrimination is a little ridiculous, when you come right down to it. You'll have to learn to throw things away like the better criminals do."

Miss Shaw opened her pretty mouth again. "But I still don't understand how—"

"—he did it? Very easily. He took the original tape home with him, pretending it had been stolen. He thought he might put it to some use. The first tape showed how hard he was practicing to get the voice right. I was in New York a few days ago investigating the disappearance of another basketball player. La Salle had probably heard the news report that Ellis

144

Decker was missing. He called my answering service here and they told him my hotel number in New York. When he called, I still hadn't found Decker, and it was easy to think the same Chinese caller whom I had associated with my friend Gonzaga's death was at it again. The fact that he recorded the dual conversation merely shows his dedication and thoroughness. Undoubtedly he was planning other calls, and the more he had of me, the better he hoped to get."

"But why would he do that?" the Shaw kid asked.

"I thought I told you. He hates private investigators. His wife hired one. It cost him the marriage, a bundle of money and a warm outside relationship. It could have ruined his reputation too. He got off lucky, but he nursed his grudge instead of appreciating his luck."

The shaggy-haired girl glanced sympathetically at her boss. La Salle ignored her and concentrated on looking sick. "You're saying he did all that business with the tapes just to even things with you because you're another investigator?"

I shrugged. "I happened along. The setup was right down his alley."

Miss Shaw shook her head. Her hair didn't bounce. "You're only guessing. What if Dr. La Salle did do all you said but for a different motive—to get the killer off the track? He might have been planning a trap to catch the killer for you. This field is his specialty, you know. He knows more about it than almost anybody."

"You might have a point," I said, "were it not for exhibit number two." I showed her the item La Salle had hidden in the boot beneath his bed. "It's a .22 pistol. It shoots real bullets, not as dangerous as a larger-caliber gun, but it still can kill people."

My other pocket produced a spent bullet. "This bullet came from this gun belonging to Dr. La Salle. It was fired at me and a young lady at the airport the other morning before I took off for New York. Luckily, it missed us both."

Her answer proved that science was only her hobby. "You took another girl to New York with you?"

I shook the old sad head. "No. She offered to drive me from my place to the airport."

She sniffed and went back to logic. "And Dr. La Salle fired at you? But why would he do that? Furthermore, assuming he did, how would he know you were going to the airport just then, not to mention being near your specific airline terminal at that precise time?"

"I don't think he shot to kill," I said. "Merely to add more confusion. To remind me of the original tape threat that somebody was out to get me. As for knowing the exact time, he might have got that from my answering service, that I had just left and where I was going. He could have made better time getting down there."

"That sounds awfully convenient," she said.

"Maybe he's got my phone bugged. That's convenient too. People in the tape business are pretty good at that. But it might even have been coincidence—that he happened to be in the parking lot across the street when we pulled up. He chose that moment impulsively to shoot."

La Salle staggered, holding his head. "I—I—think I'd better sit down . . ."

I yanked a chair forward for him. "Be my guest." As he lowered himself into it, I yanked the chair away. La Salle fell heavily to the floor. His face was choleric with rage as he looked up at me.

I nodded. "You're right. It was a cheap trick. But so was what you did. By trying for your own kind of hate-revenge against a private investigator, you only confused and delayed me, giving a dangerous killer more time to get around and do his own kind of sick-hate work."

I yanked him up by his collar and dumped him into the chair. "Before I forget, there's something else you should know. I caught up with the mystery man on the tape. His name is Frankie Wu. I asked him where he was born. He told me, and he ought to know. Southern province of China. Yunnan."

That's about all you can do to a sick man. Hit him where it hurts.

The shaggy-haired girl was suddenly at my side, her hand on my sleeve. "You've been awfully impressive tonight, Mr. Roper. But there's something I simply must tell you."

"What?" I asked.

The Giant Kill

Her fingers dug into my arm. "It's Saturday night and I'm hungry."

I glanced at my watch. "Fine. I can take you to dinner. I don't have to kill anybody for a few hours."

Twenty-three

It was almost four days since Jo-Jo Gonzaga had been blown off his balcony. Somehow the banks still had not reclaimed it or the IRS people snatched it for back taxes. The million-dollar lean-to shack remained without its rightful owner, tenanted only by Gonzaga's man Little Freddy, who was staying on to keep it straight and feed the dogs until the lawyers got in their last licks.

I called him about the idea I had. He thought the record I asked about was upstairs in Gonzaga's bedroom, and I held the phone while he checked. He came back on saying it was, and I told him what to do with it. He asked what else he could do to help and I decided that too. He agreed to take the night off, leave the front door unlocked and a few lights on. I was stumped when he asked if I was going to take the killer when I got there, because I honestly didn't know.

I drove down to Inglewood. Boxing was over for the night and so was fighting to drive away out of the Forum parking lot. There was room for everybody now all over again, and I figured that included me, found a space and parked.

A few maintenance people finished what they were doing and came out. Some of the early night-duty guards started coming off the line too, and then I saw Power. His patrol pistol was still inside his hip holster, barely covered by his open and flapping windbreaker. He wiped his lips with the back of his hand, looked up at the stars in the sky, and took a breath of the cool night air. Then he walked over toward his car, limping badly, long arms swinging, looking a lot like some gaunt and rangy cowpoke.

He saw me and stopped. I hand-waved him over, and he didn't hurry. I figured the night wind had taken some of the edge off his whiskey breath, and leaned my head out of the car window when he drew closer.

"Do they let you carry your pistol when you're off duty?" I asked.

"Sure. Why the hell not? I'm a frigging guard, ain't I? Well, after what happened to me the other night when those three pals of yours jumped me, I'm taking this baby with me. Covering this lot ain't everything. I'm using it for my own protection."

"That's good," I said. "I've got a tough job to do tonight. If you're willing to help, I can use you. I need a good back-up man I can depend on."

He grinned sourly and rubbed his scalp. "What's this all about?"

"Remember how you felt about Gonzaga's killer? You were willing to do anything to help me catch up with him?"

"Well, sure."

"I've got him all staked out and set up for tonight. I'm seeing him in a little while. There's a chance he might get away. But if you come along, I can nail him. He won't be expecting you there. Okay?"

Power took a deep breath and pulled his holster down a little. He rubbed his big hands together and blew on them. "You betcha," he said. "Your car?" I nodded and opened the door on the other side. Power hobbled around the hood and got in. "You mean you know who the sonofabitch is?"

I turned the key and got the car started, and eased it back in reverse. "He had me faked out all along. But there's no mistake now. Everything fits and he's got to be the killer."

Power rubbed his hands on his chest. "All right, already. Stop bein' so goddamn mysterious. Who the hell is it?"

"A man so rich nobody would ever figure him for murder."

"No kidding? Okay, who?"

"His name is Jules Belmont."

149

"Belmont?"

"Jules Belmont. He's got a yacht down at the marina. Ever hear Gonzaga mention his name?"

"Maybe—I ain't sure. You say he's rich?"

"In the millions. Maybe it's billions."

Power gaped. "And you're telling me he's the guy knocked off Gonzaga?"

"It's hard to believe. I wasted a lot of time running around in circles because it didn't make sense to me either."

Power looked down at me shrewdly. "What changed your mind?"

"Two things. One was the death of Decker . . ."

"But hold it—Decker was killed in New York."

I smiled thinly. "There are ways to get there. Belmont can afford them. He can afford to charter an airplane all to himself."

Power shrugged. "Okay, maybe. What's the other?"

"His ex-wife was found murdered earlier tonight—a singer known as Joanna Burton."

Power shook his head. "Honest—I don't get it. What's the connection?"

"Try your memory—maybe it will come to you."

Power scowled. "Come on, what are ya giving me—" Then suddenly he clapped his hands together. "Jesus, what's the matter with me, anyway! I get it now, sure—that's the broad Gonzaga was tooling with lately! Sure—the singer!"

"All right," I said. "Do you have it now?"

Power scraped his feet and scowled some more. "Well—I mean—not exactly. Maybe I'm dumb, but I don't see—"

"Okay, I couldn't see it either. I was at his plant the other day—in El Segundo. He was moving some things around and accidentally knocked a picture over. It was one of the blond ex-Joanna. He got rid of her a few years ago. He said it was because she was too expensive."

Power nodded. "Okay. Sure. That's the way some blondes are. Not to mention most broads. So what?"

"Look at it the other way. What if he lost her—and didn't like the idea. I told you he was a very wealthy man. Suppose you've got all that money, and then you find out it doesn't do

150

you that much good—you can't even hold on to the one thing in your life you really want."

"You mean the broad? He was still hooked on her?"

"Right. He's no chicken, in his fifties. And he looks as if he doesn't have much longer to go. He's a tough ruthless man in business, I understand. Won't buckle under. Wants to win every big deal."

"Yeah. I heard of those guys."

"Okay. You remember Gonzaga's life style. He never believed in keeping anything he did a secret."

"No question. The biggest stud in town—and proud of it."

"So it's no surprise if Belmont finds out who's balling his pretty little Joanna. Right? And to really rub Belmont's nose in it, she picks a big Mex for her lover! *The biggest around!*"

Power's eyes popped. "Hey—I getcha now! The old guy—he don't like Chicanos messing around with his chick, even if they're divorced."

"I hear that's not too unusual. Now here comes the tie-up. Those three hoods you ran into—the mysterious Chinese cookie—they were tied up with Belmont. What I never told you before was they picked me up and whipsawed me—brought me down to Belmont's boat. The Chinaman gave me the order then—I had to stop Gonzaga from playing in the play-off series. If I didn't, he was dead. If he played, he got it. Incidentally, I was part of the deal. If he played, I was supposed to get it too."

Power lit a cigarette and blew smoke. "So that was what that was all about. But—again I don't get it—what's the series games got to do with it?"

I lit my own cigarette off Power's. "Belmont's a big gambler. He was in heavy on the games. If Gonzaga didn't play, he stood to make a lot of money."

"Okay. Yeah, it figures. Only—"

"Only he was supposed to be kept out of it. Wu was the front man who would take the rap if anything went wrong. Now Gonzaga does play—and what happens?"

Power snapped his fingers. "I getcha. The old man blows his head off and nobody knows the real reason?"

"That's it. Then he goes after Decker in New York. If you

151

can't guess why, it's for the same reason. Decker was already beginning to mouth it up he intended filling Jo-Jo's shoes all around. He was ready to move in on Joanna when the team returned from New York."

Power stroked his long angular jaw. "You mean, this Belmont wasn't going to sit around and be a patsy for a brown boy shacking up with his baby." He thought about it and nodded. "So he can afford not to sit around and worry—he goes right after him, nails him, and then he don't have to worry about it."

"That's it. So far, he had himself covered pretty well. Nobody knew where he was or what he was doing. He knocks them both off, and he's back in town, back in business."

"Smart cookie!"

"That's what he thought, too. But somebody was smarter. Can you guess?"

Power scowled some more and shrugged. "You?"

I laughed. "No way. He still had me faked out. But he couldn't fool Joanna. She smelled a rat, figured out who had a pretty good reason for killing Gonzaga and Decker—and tried to nail him on it."

"You mean—like blackmail?"

"Belmont only *thought* he knew how expensive Joanna was. Now she started to lay it on him—she must have told him she could pin it on him—and there it is. You know how blackmail is. Once you start paying off and they get their hooks in you, you're gone. Maybe I didn't mention it before, Belmont for all his money happens to be a miser. He hates spending a dime. Now he finds out what it will cost him, and what can happen if he tells her to go to hell! She might have something on him, after all. He doesn't have any choice now. He does something she never expects—he kills her!"

Power was rubbing his hands together excitedly. "No kidding! Jesus! Yeah, it figures!"

"Another thing I didn't tell you, Power, was—I was there! I saw what he did to her."

Power stared. "You mean you were there when he knocked her off? You saw—"

"No, not the killing. I was still in New York then. I mean I

saw her body tonight. I don't know how many swings he took at
her, but he couldn't have missed many. I've seen a lot of blood
before, but this one was special. He got it all out of his system.
All the love he had for her turned into all the hate for what she
was doing to him."

Power rubbed his hair. "Yeah, I guess. But okay, so you
know he did it. So what's the problem? Don't the fuzz know?"

I gripped his arm. "Listen, Power. I feel sorry for her just
like I'd feel sorry for anybody else who got it that way. But she's
not my problem. I swore I'd get the man who killed Gonzaga. I
figured out a way I can get Belmont tonight. I thought maybe
you'd be interested too."

"Okay, sure. Whatever you say, Roper."

"I don't want him to get away. He's clever. He's got it
planned now that some other guy will take the rap for him."

"How's that?"

"He's no dummy. He's got a list of all the men who fell for
his Joanna. There's got to be one guy in there who hated
Gonzaga's guts as much as he did. Belmont's rich. The fuzz
might find the other guy easier to send up."

"Ain't that always the way," Power said morosely. "Well,
what the hell can you and me do about it?"

"You've been to Gonzaga's house?"

"Well, yeah . . . a couple of times. A few parties."

"I asked Belmont to meet me there. He wasn't too anxious
until I told him Joanna cut a different kind of record before she
died, spilling all she had on him. She sent it to me because she
knew I was Gonzaga's friend and would avenge him."

"A record? I thought they put those things on tape."

I shrugged. "Records are her thing, remember. She could
have done it late one night at her recording studio. But I told
Belmont I'd play it for him tonight. And if he brought along a lot
of cash, say fifty grand—I might be willing to let him have it."

Power whistled. "Fifty grand!"

"That's only peanuts to him. If he wasn't such a tightwad,
I'd press for more. I told him Gonzaga's houseman was taking
the night off and we'd have the place all to ourselves. He finally
agreed on a time, and it's all set."

Power waggled his head. "Wow! That ought to be fun. But

after what you told me—ain't you taking a big chance? Remember what he did to Joanna for trying the same deal."

The Brentwood hills were dark and quiet as I eased the car around the last turn. "That's why I asked you to come along. You're a security guard, aren't you? I might need a little protection."

Power grinned. "Okay. When's the big meeting?"

"It's about to start."

Gonzaga's big dogs were quiet, probably sleeping off a big dinner. Power trailed me slightly as we walked up to the house. He limped badly and couldn't conceal it.

"I thought that steel brace gave your knee more support," I said.

"It did," Power said disgustedly, "but I twisted the goddamn knee. The damn ligament must'a sprung again and swelled up. I had to take the brace off—it was cutting into it." He squinted across the circular driveway. "I guess we're early. He ain't here yet."

"That's the way I planned it. We'll have a little time to get organized first. I'll show you where I think you ought to be stationed. See what you think."

"Okay." Power planted his feet together and craned his head up. The surrealistic two-million-buck reminder of a dream jutted to the stars. "What a layout!" Power breathed. "And the poor sonofabitch ain't even alive to enjoy it."

The fifteen-foot-high front door was unlocked. The rooms downstairs were dark save for one discreetly lit lamp which cast a dim glow. The rest was in shadow. I touched Power's arm and felt him twitch. "Upstairs," I whispered. "We're meeting him in Gonzaga's bedroom."

The wall-to-wall carpeting was a prowler's dream. If the stairs creaked, we didn't know it. As we approached the landing to the second-floor bedroom, Power hesitated. Soft music was coming from inside the room. "What the hell is that?" he asked hoarsely.

"Little Freddy still lives here," I said. "He must have forgotten to turn the stereo set off when he went out."

Her voice was warm and true, as I remembered it, even if she was something else again. The psychedelic lighting glowed dimly in soft greens and purples. Our images reflected crazily in the angled mirrors. The huge circular bed was all made up, with nowhere to go. I resisted an impulse to jab at the electronic panel, to open the roof for a look at the skies.

Power had frozen near the drawn curtains leading to the small low-railed terrace. I pulled them aside. A pale beam of moonlight brushed across the carpet. I threw the big doors open. A light breeze gently moved the curtains.

Joanna Burton's voice was as light and gentle: "It doesn't matter any more / Who's right or wrong / We've been lovers much too long / Making believe is a wasting lie / Each time we try it lately / I want to die . . ."

I let her sing a little longer, because she was going to be dead a long, long time and this was all she had going for her any more. The song ended and the record dropped. The automatic system put another one on. It was one of hers, her voice gin-husky and caressing, the way you like to hear it in bars.

Power stood rigidly at the curtain line, his eyes shifting over the terrace wall along the horizon. The hills were masked in shadowy blackness. I didn't tell him he had nothing to fear tonight from a madman's bullet out there.

He gestured impatiently, his hands difficult to see in the dark bedroom. "Can that music, will ya? I wanna think."

I moved the player-arm lever to off. The turntable arm lifted and swung away. The music stopped. I walked closer to Power. He seemed reluctant to step into the moonlight flooding the open doorway of the terrace.

"Where you're standing now seems pretty good," I said. "The room's dark and Belmont wouldn't spot you behind the curtains. If that doesn't suit you, maybe the terrace would be just as good. He wouldn't see you unless he stepped out and looked around. I'd see to it that he didn't do that."

Power thumbed his jaw with one hand. His other flirted nervously with the gun handle off his right hip. "I don't know yet. There's somethin' about this bugs me, only I don't know what, yet. How much time we got left before he shows up?"

I turned my watch crystal up to the moonlight. "He should

be along in a few minutes. But from here, we'd see him park his car and walk up the drive. You'd have plenty of time even then to pick your hiding place."

"Maybe that's what's bugging me," Power said. "You said you wanted a back-up man. If that's what you want, I ought to be waiting downstairs. That way, if he knocks you over, somehow I can still stop him before he gets out and away."

"You're right," I said immediately. "That's why I wanted to leave that part up to you. Naturally, I don't expect him to knock me over, but you're right—you never can tell about those things."

Power grunted. "He ain't no dummy. Don't forget, if he knocked Joanna off for trying blackmail on him, like you say, he can be ready for you. Chances are he'd come packing a gun."

"It's possible," I admitted. "That's why I told you I was glad to see you wearing yours."

"How about you? You got one on you?"

I shook my head and turned my coat open, pulling it back to show him how clean I was. "Not tonight. I don't need a gun to stop Belmont. He's a little old man. I can blow him over."

"Yeah?" Power breathed doubtfully. "Well, maybe so." He gave me the horse snicker. "I forgot you're the pro at this— you're the goddamn hero."

"There's one in every crowd," I said. "I expect Belmont to crack right away. All I've got to do is point out this spot here between us. That's where Gonzaga died, right there near your feet. He was standing out on his terrace looking up at the sky when four Magnum bullets hit him in the chest."

"Is that how it happened?" Power said. "If you're right, Belmont must be a damn good shot. You better watch yourself, Roper."

"Screw him," I said. "Anybody who would knock off a man that way, hidden way the hell out there in the hills, wouldn't have the guts to kill somebody up close to him."

"Maybe you're right," Power said. "Still, like you said, you can't always tell. Come to think of it, how close do you figure he was to Decker when he got it?"

"You've got a point there," I admitted. "He was very close. I figure he had to be standing right behind him when he pulled the wire around Decker's throat and choked him to death."

Power was shaking his head stubbornly. "That don't figure neither. You told me he was a little guy, this Belmont. Decker was even bigger than I am, close to seven feet. How the hell is a little guy gonna get that close and be able to put a wire noose around a guy's neck he can't even reach? Did he bring a chair along to stand on, maybe?"

"As a matter of fact, that point has been bothering me, too. The more I think of it now, Belmont *couldn't* have done it. As you say, he was too small, for one thing."

Power sounded puzzled. "Not Belmont?"

"I had so much on him, I never took the trouble to add the little pieces up," I said. "The only way he could have brought Decker low enough for the wire noose was to punch him in the gut. That might have buckled Decker and brought him down to Belmont's size." I thought about it, picturing it, and had to shake my head. "No good. Decker would have gone down on his face that way. He was found on his back. A pitchfork had been stabbed several times into his chest. No, it's no good, Power. Decker weighed about two-forty—too much for a guy like Belmont to turn over."

"So then, what the hell are you talking about? You said you had him down for it all."

"I was stupid—not thinking."

Power snapped his fingers. "Hold it—I got it! Those three hoods! The ones you told me were after Gonzaga from the start. They were big guys—they'd have no problem."

"No. They were big enough but they weren't around."

"How do you know?"

"Decker was killed Thursday evening in New York. Those three guys were in Nuevo Laredo, Mexico, that night."

Power smirked. "Oh, yeah? How d'ya know that for sure?"

"Because that's where they were when I caught up with them."

"Maybe they got away."

"No chance. I killed them."

Power cleared his throat. "All three?"

"They were all together. That made it easier."

"Jesus—you don't fool around, do you?"

I shrugged modestly. "Maybe I got lucky."

Power took a tentative step toward the terrace to look out, keeping well behind the curtains. The little bar table was to his right, against the wall. It was still loaded with Gonzaga's choice stock and I wondered when Power would notice and start free-loading.

His mind was still too busy to think of boozing. "Wait a second. There was another guy you mentioned—the Chinaman who ran the three musclemen. How about him?"

"No, he was down in Mexico too. He managed to get away, but he came straight up to L.A. That's where he's been since."

Power shrugged his wide shoulders. "Okay, then—you said Joanna had it all figured out Belmont did it all. If Belmont knocked her off because he thought she had too much on him, he must've believed it. Hell, *he* oughtta know!"

"Maybe he had other reasons he never told me about. But there's one other possibility for Decker's killer—for instance, you could have killed him."

Power snickered. "You gotta be kidding."

I turned my head toward the record player at the other end of the room. "Maybe I ought to play that damn record of Joanna's to see what she really has."

"Let's get back to me, meanwhile. We can do the record later."

"I figure you killed Decker because it was only natural for you to follow up after you shot down Gonzaga."

I was close enough to Power to see his chest raise as he took a deep breath. "Gonzaga? What the hell are you talking about now? Are you nuts or something? Gonzaga was a friend of mine. I didn't know Decker that well, but, Jesus—Gonzaga? I'd'a given my right arm for him after what he done for me."

"And you did—only there was a big Mauser rifle in it at the time. Sure, Gonzaga was a friend of yours, and sure, he did a hell of a lot for you. But he did a whole lot more that you didn't like, that you never did forgive him for. That's why you killed him."

Power was shaking his head, keeping it down against his chest. "You're honest-to-God nuts!"

"What he did was take your girl away from you—Joanna Burton. I know that. Even Belmont remembers she went with somebody like you before she latched on to Gonzaga. You were willing to give up your wife and kids for her, but she told you to get lost. Every night you saw her with Gonzaga, it ate you up inside a little more.

"Then, when I came to you at the Forum and told you about the plot—the three guys who were after Gonzaga if he didn't stay out of the series—you had the perfect alibi. You knew he was playing at the risk of his life. That was the chance you always wanted. All you had to do was stake yourself outside his house in the cover of the hills. You knew his habits, how he liked his balcony. When you knocked him off, you knew I already had my suspects—the Chinaman and his three big musclemen."

Power moved his head just enough to spit out on the balcony. "Jesus, are you ever nuts! No way, I tell you."

"You kept shoving those three guys at me, putting them right up in the front of my mind. That Wednesday night, when you came over to my place, you said to talk, remember? You told me the same three guys beat you up, knocked you down, told you to tell me to lay off or I'd be getting more of it."

"Sure. You saw yourself what they done to me. Christ, I was bleedin' like a pig."

"That part fits. But those three guys couldn't have done it. They braced me last Sunday night. The Chinese leader Wu called me Monday night to warn me again. But it was all a bluff. They were doing it as part of a favor for Belmont, to help him win a bet. After calling me Monday night, they all went down to Mexico. If you want my guess, you either fell down drunk and bumped your head, or you tried to make time with Joanna again, and she clobbered you with her purse or a spiked heel. Whoever did it to you, it wasn't the same three guys."

"I told you I never got a good look at them. It could'a been three other guys. Christ, that's what I draw for tryin' to do somebody like you a favor."

"Okay, I'm an ungrateful sonofabitch. Now we get to

Decker. Decker was going to make time with Joanna when he got back here from New York, he was going to fill Gonzaga's shoes now, all the way. That had to burn you, because it meant a black man cozying it up with her. You couldn't stand that any more than you could a Mex. That's why you went to New York to kill him."

"Why the hell would I want to do that? If I wanted to kill Decker, I could have waited till he got back here."

"It was trickier your way. You only work nights, so you could have taken an early morning flight to New York. Right after you saw me, Thursday morning. You've been all around the league when you played ball. You know where they room. You called Decker at the Laker hotel, got him to come out to meet you. A cabbie saw him enter the park at five. It's a short walk to the zoo house, wouldn't take long. Not much longer for you to get him inside that maintenance yard and choke him with the wire. Then the pitchfork a couple of times. You're big and strong enough for the job."

"Sure. Why would Decker be dumb enough to meet me outside?"

"He knew you were Gonzaga's friend, so he'd trust you. You could have conned him easily. It was his first series and he had to be nervous. You could have had him believing you had some of Gonzaga's playing secrets to pass on to him, maybe some out of your own playing experience. You said he was wet behind the ears, and you were probably right.

"You could have made the seven P.M. return from La Guardia. It's only a five- to six-hour flight. With the three-hour difference between New York and L.A. time, you could have knocked Decker off at five, and been back at your job at the Forum by ten-thirty or eleven. The place was jammed Thursday night for the big track meet. Nobody would know you were missing a few hours."

Power chuckled. "I suppose you can prove some of that?"

"That's the trouble. I can't prove one goddamn thing."

"Tough," he said. "We all got problems."

"Who won the 440?" I asked. "Evans?"

"Huh—I dunno."

"That goes on early. How about the half—who won the 880? Was it Billy Mills?"

"I—I forget."

"Okay. How about the sprints? They go on first. The 60, the 100—can you remember a winner? No? Maybe one of the girls—you like girls—I hear one of them made it a new 880 meet record. Little girl with pigtails."

Power was mumbling, head down, shaking it negative.

"That's kind of strange, isn't it? You're an athlete—you know them all. How come you don't remember a single event if you were there earlier."

Power slammed his fist into his other hand. "Because I was too goddamn busy, that's why. They had a helluva lot of people to take care of. I get paid for doing a security job, not watching those long-haired fags run around!"

"Seeing the way you're limping gave me the idea, Power. You don't have your steel knee-support brace because it's down at L.A. airport. When you got there, you forgot they were checking everybody now because of the skyjackers. You couldn't take a chance of running through the metal detectors and having them pull you out to question you. Then it would be on the record, that you were there. Instead you dumped it in the men's room. I saw something like it on the shelf in Security with all the other ditched props people are afraid to wear."

"You're nuts. I told you I pulled my knee. It got swollen and I had to take the goddamn brace off. What the hell are you tryin' to do to me, for Christ's sake?"

"I'm finished after I show you how you killed Joanna Burton."

"Oh, boy—I thought you had Belmont down for that one, for sure."

"He's a possible, but I like you more for the job. You killed her late Thursday after Decker—on Friday. She didn't show up for work Friday or tonight, but the medical report will figure out the time. She looked kind of stiff and cold to me earlier tonight. It didn't bother you how you went about it, and that says a lot too. You knew you couldn't hold her, she didn't want you for dust, and you couldn't stand that any more than the idea of all the blacks that she might be going in for in the future. Once she was dead, you're rid of her for good and no more worries."

"You're off your rocker, Roper. You're all talk. You can't prove one goddamn thing about any of them."

"Maybe. I didn't see you shoot Gonzaga and I haven't found the gun. Same with Joanna. No witness, no clue, yet. With Decker, I've got a little something going. There were blood-stained fingerprints on that pitchfork. When you were at my place, you left some bloody handprints on a glass. I put it away to remind me of something. Now if those prints match up, then maybe I can really prove something. Right?"

Instead of playing fair and answering me, Power whipped out his gun and belted me across the forehead. As I fell back he hit me with his other hand. I don't remember how I got to the other end of the room but that's where I was next. Blood was streaming down my eyes when I got them open. I could make out Power dimly across the room. His gun glinted in the moonlight, pointed in my direction.

I knew I had to get off my butt and do something, but my head was split, my brain was numb and fogged, and I couldn't think of a thing.

"Get up!" Power was saying. "I wanna give it to you in a place you can remember."

Numb or not, somehow I was able to surmise his intention. I knew I had studied karate somewhere and could lay out people and kill them with it, but in that line, if you can't reach somebody, you have to forget it. I couldn't even remember if I had a gun on me anywhere.

"On your feet!"

I pushed back against the wall, leaned on Gonzaga's bed and got up slowly. I still wasn't much good and fell back against the wall.

"While you're at it, get that record and toss it over. The one you say Joanna made to fix Belmont. I wanna hear it when I got time. Maybe she's got somethin' there I can use."

There wasn't any record, and I knew it if Power didn't. But it gave me something to do with my spare time while trying to get my head together. I made a show of fumbling through the stack on top and finally came up with one that felt right, the record Joanna Burton had cut, the one playing when we entered Gonzaga's bedroom.

"Okay, toss it over." His gun jerked forward again, reminding me I was still a very dead pigeon.

I stumbled as I straightened up and fell against the huge bedboard. "Come on!" Power urged. I remembered how Gonzaga had made the little bar table walk across the room, how he had pretended impatience and made it really move. I hit the double key button the way he did.

Power cursed as it bumped him from the side and his bad knee buckled. I still couldn't see him clearly and I ran the table at him again. I heard the bottles tinkle as he was pushed in front of the open doorway to the terrace. Gonzaga had moved the ceiling quietly, I recalled, and I tagged that button, too.

It must have worked because suddenly I could make out Power standing in a bright beam of moonlight pouring down from the roof. I knew I'd never have another chance and I scaled Joanna Burton's record across the room with a backhanded wrist flip. It caught Power flush, squarely under his chin, smashing his windpipe, and he staggered back. He kept stumbling backward until he hit the low terrace ledge, and then he fell over and out of sight.

Gonzaga's big dogs were hired for their bad tempers. Obviously, Power had disturbed their sleep, and if nothing else he was an intruder on the grounds, and they knew what to do about that. I heard their thunderous roars, a bleating strangled moan of terror, and then the crunching and snapping of jaws splintering bone and tearing flesh.

I staggered weakly to the terrace and looked down, but that didn't do Power any good.

Twenty-four

Camino didn't blow his stack. "Okay. We'll take your word for it. Gonzaga's dogs killed him. I don't know if we have a public defender for dogs, but I'll look into it for you."

"What about Belmont? Did you find out what he was bringing up from Mexico for Wu?"

Camino laughed. "I'm glad you mentioned Belmont. He told me he was a businessman with a respectable import and export line. Narcotics wasn't his bag because he had too much going for him."

"But, Nick—"

"If I had listened to him and believed him instead of you, then I wouldn't have felt like such a stupid horse's ass after breaking up some of those crates from Mexico."

"Oh, what did you find?"

"Maracas."

"Maracas?"

"You know, those little gourds—those things you shake—especially if you work in a marimba band."

Camino wasn't making it up.

I stared down at what appeared to be a crate full of them. Maracas.

A maraca is a percussion instrument made of a gourd. It is used in marimba bands, as Camino had said. It is a gourd-shaped rattle with beans or beads inside it, and you don't need the marimba band, you can shake them all by yourself and have that kind of fun, if that's your thing.

Camino was strutting in the warehouse, humming a brisk Latin beat, snapping his fingers together, making funny sounds with his teeth. "Ssst . . . ssst . . . sst." When he got tired of that, he picked up a couple of the maracas right out of the crate and shook them briskly in my face.

"You dance divinely," I said. "I like that rustling sound they make."

"It's the beans or beads inside them," Camino said, and then stopped dancing. He chopped a few maraca heads off. He held them in his hand and showed them to me. "Sorry. For a moment there, I thought you might be right for a change."

"They'd be awfully stupid to put the heroin inside on the top layer," I said. "How about going a little deeper?"

Camino pointed dramatically to the open crate. "It's your idea."

I dug a couple of them out. I broke them apart and there were little white balls inside. I showed them to Camino and rubbed them lightly and they fell apart into a fine white powder.

"Not a bad idea," Camino said. "So they used a little wax binder to hold the stuff together. It sure sounds like the beans and beads in the others."

"That's because he's such a good businessman," I said.

Belmont might not have been a gent completely on the level, but his scales were. Camino showed me the figures.

"We make it ninety-four pounds," he said.

"Not bad," I said.

"Roughly worth $27.3 million," he said.

"That was a great idea you had," I said, "looking into those maracas."

Camino smiled. "You're telling me!"

My head still felt terrible. "Then it was all true. Ridiculous but true. Belmont didn't have a single reason for getting involved with these jokers. He's got all the money he'll ever need and he had to stick his neck out to get a little more. Why?"

"You just told me why," Camino said. "To get a little more."

The I AM-ness twiggie didn't let the news about her uncle being such a crook throw her. "Money is the root of all evil," she said. "You promised to come to my boat and see my paintings."

"As soon as my head heals."

"You mean you were zonked again?"

"Yes, but it must be getting better because your voice sounds familiar."

When I got there she reminded me to duck my head, and I did. She had a few of her paintings rigged inside around the boat, propped up against corners.

"Very nice," I said. "Really very nice."

"I'll show you something that's really nice," she said. I turned and was aghast to see her arms high in the air. She seemed to be tugging at something, and as it gave way I saw she was taking her sweater off, pulling it over her head.

After that, I noticed she wasn't wearing anything underneath. I coughed politely, but with all that wool over her ears, she didn't hear anything.

Finally I said, "You don't know what you're doing."

She smiled. "I know. That's why I invited you over. To teach me."

About the Author

KIN PLATT was the newspaper cartoonist of the comic strip *Mr. and Mrs.* for the New York Herald Tribune Syndicate. His theatrical caricatures have also been featured in many newspapers and magazines. He is currently living in Los Angeles. He has written several popular juveniles, among them *Sinbad and Me*, which won the Edgar Award from the Mystery Writers of America for the best juvenile mystery of the year, and *The Boy Who Could Make Himself Disappear*, which was distributed as a major motion picture under the title *Baxter*. He has written four previous adult mysteries: three of them, *The Pushbutton Butterfly*, *The Kissing Gourami* and *The Princess Stakes Murder*, feature private eye Max Roper; in the fourth, *Dead as They Come*, there is Molly Mellinger, New York mystery editor and amateur detective.